BUFFALO GAL

BUFFALO GAL

Bill Wallace

Holiday House / New York

Library of Congress Cataloging-in-Publication Data
Wallace, Bill, 1947–
Buffalo gal / by Bill Wallace.
p. cm.
Summary: Fifteen-year-old Amanda's refined life in early-twentieth-
century San Francisco is disrupted when she grudgingly accompanies her mother
to the Oklahoma Territory on a crusade to save the buffalo.
ISBN 0-8234-0943-0
[1. Mothers and daughters—Fiction.   2. West (U.S.)—Fiction.
3. Bison—Fiction.]   I. Title.
PZ7.W15473Bu 1992 [Fic]—dc20 91-28243   CIP   AC

To Leonard and Mary Kay Garrison,
and to their children, Carl and Dana

BUFFALO GAL

CHAPTER 1

Who—in his right mind—would ever want to go to Oklahoma or Texas? Oklahoma wasn't even a state yet. It was still just a territory. And Texas . . . what was there in Texas? It was nothing but dust and wide-open spaces and outlaws and dirty little cow towns.

The freight train made a clickety-clack sound as we chugged over the tracks.

Maybe in fifty years, maybe around 1954 or so, civilized people might be living in Texas. I doubted it, though, from what I had seen and heard about the place. But now . . .

I glared at Mother.

She looked so prim and proper in her fine embroidered, blue-and-white-striped blouse with the high neck. Her long pleated skirt draped well below her ankles as she sat reading the book she'd brought with her from home.

Who would ever suspect? I mused. I continued to glare at her. As stylish and calm as she appeared, she had become rebellious and outrageous in the last month. Really, it had been longer than a month. It all began several years ago when Mother and Father attended a Save the Bison meeting with Ernest Harold Banes and William T. Hornaday. Banes was a writer for the *Boston Transcript*. Father had used some of Banes's articles in his newspaper in San Francisco and had become good friends with the man. Hornaday and Banes, along with some others, were trying to form what they called The American Bison Society. They spoke about how the bison was on the verge of extinction and what needed to be done to save it.

I remember when Mother and Father had come home from the meeting. Mother was most excited, especially about the fact that a very influential and popular politician named Theodore Roosevelt had agreed to be honorary president of the society, if it received enough support. Mother said she was most impressed with Mr. Roosevelt and could even picture him as president of the United States one of these days. Father did not agree, as he felt Roosevelt lacked the polish to ever be a successful candidate. For one of the few times in my young life, I agreed with Mother. I liked Mr. Roosevelt. I was glad I chose her side because he did become president three years ago.

However, Mother and Father both agreed that the American bison needed their help. That's where the trouble really started.

Through numerous telegrams and letters, Mother found some others who were interested in the bison: Major Gordon W. Lillie at Pawnee in the Indian Territory; Charles J. Goodnight in the badlands of Oklahoma Territory; and "Scotty" Philip at Fort Pierre. All of them had private herds of buffalo grazing on their large ranches. After more telegrams, Mother found that Lillie was the only one of the three men still searching for buffalo to add to his herd.

The last telegram had come six days ago. Then the first thing I knew, we were on a train bound for Texas. We'd been on one train after another, trying to get to a place in the Oklahoma Territory called Pawnee. On the Union Pacific we rode in a fine Pullman car. It was the latest in luxury and the dining car was most elegant. On the Atchison, Topeka & Sante Fe, the Pullman was a bit older and not as nice, but every bit as comfortable. When we changed trains once more to the Rock Island, the Pullman was old, drafty, and hot. But the dining car was the most beautiful thing I'd ever seen. Mother said it was called a Palace diner. It had fancy table trimmings that gleamed under the gas lights.

We made the journey because Major Lillie, in his last telegram, had agreed to accept Mother's assistance in finding a herd of buffalo and bringing it back to the safety of his ranch. Only, when we finally got to Pawnee, he wasn't there. They told us he was at a place called Fort Sill down in The Nations, which was their term for the Indian Territory. Major Lillie was trying to talk some government people there into making a wildlife preserve where the buffalo would be safe.

When we got to a place in Indian Territory called Chickasha, we found there was not yet rail service to Fort Sill, and not even passenger service to the end of the line—a tiny town called Rush Springs. Reluctant to hire a carriage, Mother insisted that the man at the depot let us ride in the freight car. Next we would spend the night in Rush Springs before proceeding on to the fort by wagon.

I wished Mother hadn't been so persistent. I sighed. With my luck, the wagon probably wouldn't even go to Fort Sill. We'd end up having to ride horses, walk, and finally swing from vines to get to the place.

And if riding in a freight car wasn't bad enough, I also had to worry about getting shot by outlaws, carried off by wild beasts, and being scalped by Indians.

I shot a blast of cool air up my forehead. I dabbed the "glow" on my brow with my silk handkerchief.

How I longed to be back in my little room at home. There were lacy curtains on the windows and an oriental carpet on the floor. I had a pink goose-down comforter on my bed. The breeze that swept across Nob Hill from the bay was cool and crisp and clean.

Even with the door open, it was hot in the old freight car. It smelled of wool blankets and chicken feathers.

I hated trains!

* * *

The clickety-clack of the steel wheels drummed again and again in my ears. Clickety-clack, clickety-clack, clickety . . . The dumb song that Grandmother had sung for me before we left was sneaking back into my head, and there was nothing I could do to drive it away.

Buffalo Gal, won't you come out tonight,
  Come out tonight, come out tonight;
Buffalo Gal, won't you come out tonight,
  And dance by the light of the moon.
I danced with the gal with a hole in her stockin'
  And her knees kept a-knockin'
  And her toes kept a-rockin';
I danced with the gal with a hole in her stockin'
  And we danced by the light of the moon.
Buffalo Gal, won't you come out tonight,
  Come out tonight, come out tonight . . .

With the palm of my hand I tapped my head, trying to knock that silly song out of my mind. Still, it kept coming back—in perfect rhythm with the clickety-clack of the train.

Grandmother always went around the house singing little songs to herself. When Mother started talking about doing something to save the buffalo from extinction, I guess it was the only song about buffalo Grandmother could think of. Songs, especially dumb ones, are as contagious as a cold.

One day when Grandmother was singing it in the parlor, I made her stop. I told her that this trip was a ridiculous idea and that I was sure the only reason Mother had decided to go hunting for buffalo was because she'd gone crazy.

Grandmother, who I had always been able to confide in and whom I trusted, just smiled and patted my head. "When you turn fifteen or so," she'd said, "your mother's *supposed* to go crazy. She'll likely stay that way until you're about twenty-one—and then you'll still have your doubts."

"I'm serious, Grandmother," I'd insisted.

"I am too," she'd mumbled back.

"But why buffalo?"

"Think it was 'sixty-seven, maybe 'sixty-eight . . . I don't remember for sure. Anyway, it was the year your grandfather and I moved here from Boston. On the Kansas Pacific Railway our train—a little lightweight locomotive called a "tin pot"—had to stop so a herd of buffalo could cross the tracks.

"There were a lot of buffalo back in those days. We waited hours for the woolly beasts to cross. Your mother was only five or so, but she was thoroughly fascinated with them, even back then. We spent a day or so in Abilene. One of the most popular tunes there was 'Buffalo Gal.' Your mother loved the song. She'd tap her little foot every time she heard it. Now, how did that go again?"

All I had really wanted to know was how to get out of going on this trip with Mother. Instead, I'd gotten this long-winded story about how Mother fell in love with some buffalo back in the olden days.

Grandmother had been no help. Father, who usually rushed to my rescue when Mother came up with these strange ideas, had been no help either.

"Your mother is a very strong willed and capable woman. For a long time you've known she's not like the mothers of your friends at Miss Plimpton's School. She's never been content to stay at home and knit or mind the servants. She helps me at the newspaper. She takes reporting duties that none of the other reporters want. She travels, and from time to time she finds a 'crusade' that she is most dedicated to.

"She has made up her mind to help save the buffalo, and there's nothing I can do to alter her decision. You might enjoy the trip—camping out under the stars. You love horseback riding. Besides, it would be good for you to get away. You spend far too much time sitting in the porch swing with that no-account, sugarcoated scoundrel Philip Montone. Next thing I know, you'll be wanting to ride around in that horseless carriage of his, too. Those things are just a frivolous plaything for the rich. Like Philip, they'll never amount to anything."

I hated my family!

Mother had gone crazy. There was no doubt in my mind about that. Mother led the way, but the rest of the house jumped right in to follow her. The whole bunch had gone crazy.

* * *

I fanned my face with the silk handkerchief.

Daddy was wrong about Philip. He was handsome, smart, and quite polished. I loved how he slicked his blond hair smooth with that sweet-smelling hair oil. He wore nothing but the finest hand-tailored clothes, and he always had a warm smile. I loved his brown eyes. Though they were set a bit close together, his eyes were pretty.

We had had plans for this summer. Philip had talked his parents into enrolling him in the Nob Hill Riding Academy, where I took English pleasure and jumping. I had been taking riding lessons for ten years, since I was five, so I promised to help Philip. We could spend hours riding. And in four short weeks, when I would turn sixteen, when I was to have my "coming out" party and could finally begin courting, he *would* take me for a ride in his shiny new horseless carriage.

A coming out party is the most important event in a young woman's life. The thought of possibly being gone from home when it was scheduled . . . I simply couldn't bear to think of such a thing.

"Do you think Philip is a no-account?"

"Yes, dear," Mother answered without bothering to take her nose out of the book she was reading.

"Do you think he's a scoundrel?"

"Yes, dear," she answered again, never taking her eyes from the book.

I hated it when Mother ignored me like that. Here she'd taken me away from my friends and from Philip and from all the plans we had made for this summer, and she wouldn't so much as listen to me. I felt a mischievous grin tugging at the corners of my mouth.

"Do you think Father will begin courting his secretary while we're gone?"

"No, dear."

Mother kept reading. She never looked up. I frowned, not quite sure about my mother.

We finally reached Rush Springs. A barefoot boy of about ten, by the name of Will, met us at the scrubby little building they called a depot. He took us and our luggage in a wagon to his "pappy's" hotel. It was a three-story, red brick building. New and clean, it was fairly nice. But the furnishings were quite modest and my bed was too hard. We had to wait forever for Will's "mommy" to heat water on her stove and bring it up to warm our bath.

Early the next morning, we climbed aboard the wagon and headed across the hot, dusty plains for Fort Sill.

I hated wagons!

CHAPTER 2

The wooden wagon seat was hard as rock. Within a mile or two of Rush Springs, my bottom and back were sore. Even my teeth seemed to crunch and grind together with each jarring bounce of the wagon as we plodded over the dry, rutted wagon path that stretched forever across the prairie.

We saw some mountains in the distance that were shrouded in haze and seemed almost blue.

"Them's the Wichita Mountains," the boy called Will announced proudly. "Oklahoma ain't got many mountains. Them's kinda short, but they's downright pretty, ain't they?"

I cringed at his words. Though he seemed somewhat bright, the poor grammar, the slang, the way the language slurred and twanged and sort of dripped from his mouth made the boy seem like a total idiot, a complete hick. I wondered if everyone in Oklahoma talked like that.

The mountains drew closer, though it seemed to take us forever to get near them.

"Fort's right over yonder," Will slurred as we rolled from a stand of tall trees along a creek to a wide, flat field. "Oughta be there right soon now."

In the distance I could see a group of men in blue uniforms about halfway across the big field. Another man on a horse galloped away from them. As he rode, he leaned down against the horse's neck. Then, sliding to the right, he fired a rifle.

I shuddered at the terrible sound. I've always hated loud noises. One time, when I was little, some balloons popped at Betty Riley's birthday party. I cried for hours. Mother and Father took me to the fireworks on the waterfront one Fourth of July. Instead of enjoying the festivities, I got sick to my stomach and threw up. Then I hid under the carriage. Like I said, I hated loud noises.

I hated trains, I hated this trip, I hated this wagon. Most of all . . .

I hated guns!

No sooner had the man fired his gun than he fell from his horse. There was a *whoompf* sound as he hit the ground and a huge cloud of dust exploded.

A loud burst of laughter came from the other men. They practically rolled on the ground, holding their sides and jumping around. A couple of the soldiers even fell to their knees.

Beside them, sitting on top of a long-legged gray horse, was another man. He had on no shirt, and in the afternoon sunlight his skin seemed almost bronze. At first, I thought he must be an Indian. But he was much too tall and slender. From all the pictures I had seen of Indians, I gathered they were short and stocky.

He was the only one of the group who wasn't laughing.

The soldier who had fallen from his horse stood up and dusted himself off.

"It ain't funny!" he roared at the group.

That only made them laugh harder. Rubbing his shoulder, the soldier picked up his rifle and started toward them. "Quit laughing. It ain't funny!"

The tall, dark-skinned man rode up to him. "You have to hook with your left leg and hold to the mane with your left hand," he called out. "Pay attention. I'll show you one last time."

With that, he dug his heels into the big gray's sides. As the horse raced at a dead-out run, the man slipped to the right side of the animal's neck. With his left leg hooked over its back and his left hand holding the mane, he pointed the rifle under the horse's neck.

A shot snapped above the sound of thundering hoofbeats. At the base of a hill, across the valley from where he rode, stood a row of four posts. On top of each one was a sandbag. A puff of dust exploded from the first when he fired. The same thing happened with the second, third, and fourth.

I hated the awful, loud sound of the rifle. Still, I was fascinated by the man's skill. I couldn't help but watch.

An instant after he fired the last shot, he spun his horse and raced back toward the group of soldiers. Just before he crashed into them he yanked the reins. His big gray horse almost sat down on its haunches as it slid to a stop.

"Most impressive," Mother whispered.

I put my hand under my chin and closed my mouth. "Yes!" I breathed.

The man didn't seem to notice the applause and cheers from the men. Nor did he pay much attention when they patted him on the back and shoulders as he swung down from his horse and went to get something next to where they stood.

He knelt and grabbed a shirt from the ground beside them. He pulled it on. No sooner had it touched his shoulders than he snatched his hat from the ground and stuck it on his head. Then, tucking in the tail of his shirt, he strapped on a pistol belt and holster. Finally he picked up a saddle and blanket.

Not once had I seen him glance toward our wagon. But as he saddled his horse, he pointed. The soldiers looked toward us. They must have thought they'd been alone with no one watching, because even as far away as we were, I could see the startled expressions on their faces when the man pointed at us.

Quickly the man swung into his saddle and rode

toward us. He did not charge us as he had the soldiers. The gray's nostrils were flared. He was used to running and was ready to go again. The man held him in. His horse came, softly.

"Mrs. Guthridge?" he asked as he swung down from the saddle and removed his hat.

Will pulled the wagon horse to a stop. He set the brake with his foot.

"Yes," Mother answered.

"Please forgive me. I was to meet you at the headquarters building. I should have been more presentable. Please pardon my appearance."

Mother smiled. "We are, perhaps, somewhat early. You have no need to apologize." She raised her eyebrows. "You must be Major Lillie?"

"No, ma'am. My name is David. I work for the major. He has been detained at the telegraph office, and has asked me to escort you to the quarters that Colonel Stewart has provided. He promises that he will join you shortly." The young man smiled, then turned to me. "And this must be your daughter, Amanda?"

I didn't answer. I only sat there, looking at him.

From a distance, because of his great skill with the rifle, I had judged him to be much, much older. Here, as he stood in front of us, I realized he was just about the same age as me.

Besides—he was quite handsome.

He had a broad, soft smile and the darkest blue eyes . . .

So instead of saying, "Yes, I am Amanda Guthridge,"
I sat there, my mouth flopped open like a total idiot's,
and stared at him.

When I didn't answer, his blue eyes turned back to
Mother. "If you would follow me, please."

Suddenly, my cheeks felt so hot they almost hurt.
As he led the way back through the trees I could feel
the red sweeping across my face. I had made such a
fool of myself. Why didn't I speak? I could have at
least said "Yes, I'm Amanda," but all I had done was
look at him.

Fort Sill was not at all like I'd expected. Instead of
being built of tall logs with guard towers at each corner, the fort was made of stone. It was a low, rambling
structure. As we drew closer I could see small slits
built into the rock walls—places from which a man
could aim a rifle and still be protected by the stone.

There was a corral next to the fort, then other buildings in the distance. A little stone church with a stee-
ple stood near the crest of a hill. Beyond it was a big
two-story house. Will pointed to it.

"Headquarters," he drawled. "That's where I got to
bring this here sack of mail and them blankets, when
we get y'all's stuff unloaded."

David led us to a small line of houses, and as Mother
and I tried to stretch the soreness out of our backs, he
and Will unloaded our baggage.

I should have said something to him. I should have
at least smiled, instead of just staring with my mouth
open.

Not only was he tall and handsome, but he was very polite. Although I could still detect a Southern drawl and a bit of a twang in his voice, his speech was quite proper and refined. Maybe he hadn't noticed how silly I had acted.

If I had only known then what a rude person he was, what a total hick, I wouldn't have even given him a second thought.

CHAPTER 3

"Bet she ain't nothin' but a spoiled brat! I bet she can't even dress herself. Bet she's got maids back home that puts her clothes on for her and even help her go to the bathroom. She probably don't know the front end of a horse from the back. Bet she can't even ride. She's just a baby."

When I heard the boy named David say that, I could have killed him. He had seemed so refined when talking with Mother. Now I realized he was nothing but a two-faced hick. If I had had a club in my hand, I would have leaped through the window and beat him over the head. Instead, I pressed myself deeper into the corner of the little house and gritted my teeth so hard, I could hear them grinding inside my head.

* * *

The two boys had taken us to a line of small houses. Our cabin was clean, with fresh-painted walls. There were screens on the windows to keep out the flies and let in the breeze.

Much to my dismay, there were no servants. A bit disgruntled, I began to help Mother unpack our clothes. That's when I saw the boy named Will motion for David to follow him around the side of the cabin. I crept into the front room and hid in the corner, next to the window where they stood.

"They seem like nice enough folks," Will had said. I'd heard David grunt.

"The girl's kinda pretty, don't you think?" Will had asked.

That's when David had said what he did.

I pressed myself deeper into the corner, squinting so much that I could barely see. I bit at the corner of my bottom lip.

"Major Lillie's coming!" a voice called from the front of the house.

When I heard the two boys moving away from the window, I darted back to the room where Mother was unpacking our bags. Still mad, I yanked open my steamer trunk and flung one of my dresses at the little closet beside the bed.

"Is everything all right, Amanda?"

I didn't answer Mother. I just grabbed another dress and threw it at the closet.

"I know it's been a long trip, dear," she soothed. "I realize you're tired—"

"It's not that," I snapped. "It's that stupid boy. That one called David. I can't stand him."

Mother didn't say any more. Neither did I. She walked around the foot of the bed and picked up the two dresses I had thrown. She smoothed them out and hung them on the wooden rod in the closet. Despite the fury that pounded inside me, I forced myself to calm down.

I *was* acting like a baby, slinging my clothes and having Mother pick up after me. I sat on the edge of the bed and rested my chin in my hands.

A knock came at the door.

Mother went to the front of the guest house. I waited in the doorway.

A man stood just outside the screen. He was dressed in Western garb—a tall, straw hat drawn to a peak at the top, a leather shirt, and brown trousers. A long, drooping mustache hung from his upper lip and his face was dark and wrinkled.

"Mrs. Guthridge." He swooped his hat from his head and bowed as Mother opened the screen door. "I'm Major Gordon Lillie, United States Cavalry, retired."

Mother held out her hand.

"Mrs. Ruben Guthridge. It's a pleasure to meet you, sir."

"The pleasure is mine," he said, taking her hand and kissing the back of it as would a true gentleman of

San Francisco. When he released her hand, Mother opened the screen door wider.

"Won't you come in?"

"I would love to visit a moment," Major Lillie said, "but I must hurry back to the telegraph office. We've had some last-minute complications that might affect our plans. We may have to cancel or postpone our trip, but . . ."

"I'm sure it's nothing that cannot be overcome." Mother's voice was stern as she cut him off.

Major Lillie cleared his throat.

"Yes. At any rate, I am sure you and your daughter are weary from your long journey and wish to freshen up. The fort commander, Colonel Stewart, and his wife would like you to come for supper at their house tonight. This would give me time to obtain more information from the telegraph office and will give you a moment or two to rest. If it is agreeable, I will send a carriage for you about six. We should have adequate time after supper to discuss the problems that have arisen."

Mother stepped back inside and closed the screen.

"We shall be ready at six," she said. Her voice had that same snap to it that she used on me when I didn't mind her.

Major Lillie put on his hat and went back to his horse. Mother stormed into the room and started yanking things out of her trunk. Now it was my turn to pick up after her as she slung her clothes at the little closet.

"Problems that have arisen," she muttered as she stomped around the bedroom. "Just like a man. Lets us take a week-long train trip, bounce across the country on a freight wagon, finally get here, and then . . . *then* tells us that 'problems have arisen.' " She threw another outfit at the closet. "If he thinks I'm the kind of person to tuck my tail and run back home . . . well . . . he's got another thing coming. . . . We'll just see about this little problem. . . ."

Mother kept muttering and throwing her clothes around.

I didn't say a word.

Colonel Stewart's home was not as elegant as the houses on Nob Hill, but it was still quite lovely. The living room was furnished with overstuffed chairs and sofas covered with fine material of the latest patterns. The dining room was dominated by an enormous oak table and chairs. Mrs. Stewart told us that her mother brought them over from England in 1860. When Mrs. Stewart and her husband were transferred from Washington, she had them shipped, along with the piano I had noticed in the living room.

I was seated at the big oak table next to Mother. The boy named David was across from me, and Mrs. Stewart was on my left. She spent most of dinner leaning across me to talk with Mother about the newest fashions in San Francisco. She said that when she was in Washington, she kept abreast of all the latest trends, but out here in the West it was difficult to get word of what was happening in the rest of the world.

While David was busy eating, I glanced at him. I was very careful not to let him catch me.

He had made me so mad earlier, I wanted to scream. Now I was somewhat unsettled and nervous in his presence. When we were seated at the table, I hardly recognized him. David did not look at all like he had when we'd first met. Instead of wearing his buckskin shirt and Western hat, he was dressed in a black suit, crisp white shirt, and black tie. His clothing was not even the slightest bit wrinkled. Much to my surprise, his manners were very polished as well. I knew it was simply an act to impress people, just as he had used proper English when he first spoke to Mother. He knew which fork to use and sat very straight and correctly—although I did catch him sopping the gravy from his mashed potatoes with his bread.

Colonel Stewart sat next to him. He spoke often, and so as not to be impolite I would look up at him when he talked. But I also watched David out of the corner of my eye.

His eyes were blue—just as I had thought. His skin was much darker than the colonel's, and I noted his cheekbones seemed a bit higher and sharper. His hair, although very clean and combed, still had a wildness to it—as if it had a mind of its own.

Once, I caught him staring at me. When I looked up, he quickly averted his eyes. During the entire meal, he didn't say a single word.

As we finished, Mother offered to help the colonel's wife clear the table. Mrs. Stewart said that some of the enlisted men's wives had helped with the meal and would take care of the dishes.

"I hear that you and Major Lillie have some business to discuss," she added. "Why don't we adjourn to the living room with the gentlemen? While they have their coffee and cigar, perhaps you and Amanda would join me in a lemonade?"

Mother kind of rocked back from the table, just like Major Lillie had done, and patted her stomach.

"I can't speak for Amanda," she said with a smile, "and I certainly do not wish to shock anyone, but I'd just as soon have some coffee and a cigar. It's been some time since I've had a good cigar."

Mrs. Stewart's eyes flashed. She caught herself quickly and straightened. "I'll have the girls bring the coffee," she said, motioning us toward the living room.

The others at the table gasped. They were every bit as shocked as Mrs. Stewart had been. Still, with the exception of David, whose blue eyes looked as big around as his plate, everyone managed to regain his composure.

I didn't catch myself as quickly as the rest of our companions. I stared at my mother with my mouth open so wide, a horse and carriage could have fit inside it. When everyone else got up and started for the living room, I just sat there, glaring at her.

I couldn't believe my mother would say something like that. After all the times she'd fussed at Grandmother for smoking, I just couldn't imagine . . .

What really got me, what almost made me fall over in a dead faint, was when she actually took the cigar from the box that Colonel Stewart offered her. Then she chomped off the end of it and spit it into the open fireplace.

CHAPTER 4

Except for the fine silk gown she wore, my mother reminded me of some sailor on the San Francisco waterfront. The other people in the room, although trying hard to act like they didn't notice her unheard-of behavior, were quite shocked.

Mother puffed calmly on the big brown cigar. Not once did she cough or allow her eyes to water. A time or two, she even talked with the horrid-looking thing stuck in the side of her mouth. She slugged down her steaming hot coffee without even flinching, and asked for seconds.

I wanted to die. I wished I could just melt into the chair where I sat and disappear so no one could ever see me again.

Finally Mother plopped down in the middle of one of the overstuffed couches. She draped her arms across the back of the sofa, like an eagle spreading its wings.

"Now, Major Lillie," she began. "What is this 'little problem' that might cause our trip to be postponed or canceled?"

It was hard to understand her, with the cigar stuffed in the corner of her mouth.

Major Lillie studied her for a long moment. Then a soft smile came to his face. With his thumb, he brushed at his long, drooping mustache.

"First, Mrs. Guthridge," he said, leaning forward to put his cigar down in an ashtray, "let me assure you that the problem has nothing to do with you, nor the fact that you are a woman. Since you first contacted me, I have had numerous occasions, both by telegram and personal letter, to correspond with your husband. I fully believe his assurances that you are strong enough and determined enough to make a trip into the hill country of Texas and would be able to handle most any hardship that might occur along the way—"

"Your point, sir," Mother cut him off.

Major Lillie cleared his throat.

"My point, ma'am, is that there is no need to impress me. If you find the cigar distasteful . . . well, you don't have to smoke it. As I said, the problem has nothing to do with the fact that you're a woman."

Mother took another puff.

"What, exactly, is the problem?"

Major Lillie twirled the tip of his mustache between his thumb and finger.

"Yesterday I received word of a shipment of buffalo

being transported to a stockyard at Omaha. They're to be fattened on corn for a couple of months, then slaughtered for Christmas dinners.

"Were they cattle instead of buffalo, I would be content to wait a month or so before traveling to Omaha to try and purchase them. But as buffalo have a tendency to tear up things—such as stock pens, cattle chutes, stockyard workers—I'm afraid that the company's plan to fatten them up on corn will soon be replaced with the workers' butchering them quite quickly.

"In other words, if I don't get there very soon, they'll probably be dead."

Mother seemed to relax a bit. She brought her arms from the back of the sofa and placed her hands in her lap. Then she took the cigar from her mouth and laid it in the ashtray.

"It is a very fine cigar," she said to Colonel Stewart. "Virginia tobacco, isn't it?"

Colonel Stewart's smile was so wide, he almost seemed to chuckle. "Yes, Mrs. Guthridge. But as with most Virginia cigars, they do get a bit stout about halfway down."

Mother smiled.

"Yes, I noticed." She picked some of the tobacco from the tip of her tongue and turned to Major Lillie. "So what you are saying, Major Lillie, is that you are planning to postpone the trip to Texas not because you fear for Amanda's or my safety, but because you have to go to Omaha?"

"That's exactly right, ma'am. If I don't get to 'em quick, they're gone."

"How long are we talking about?"

Major Lillie shrugged. "Two weeks, at the least. Perhaps as much as a month or two if the folks in Omaha want to be hard-nosed about trading. They supposedly have about twenty head of buffalo. I plan to ship forty head of cattle and see if they'll trade straight up. If not, well . . ."

"Have you considered sending one of your men to handle the trading so you could be free to go on the trip as we had planned?"

He nodded.

"Yes, ma'am. David here—" He motioned with his cigar, then suddenly stopped. "I'm sorry. I know David helped you to your quarters, but have you been properly introduced?

Mother shook her head. "We've met, but not formally."

Instantly Major Lillie stood. The boy jumped to his feet too.

"Mrs. Guthridge, please forgive my ill manners. I should have done more than *assume* you had been introduced," Major Lillie said, moving toward her. "This is David Talltree."

David shook hands with Mother, then turned back to his chair.

He *is* an Indian, I told myself. He has to be, with a name like David Talltree. Then I shook my head. No. Indians aren't that tall. Besides, they don't have blue eyes, do they?

"David's grandparents were part of a wagon train to Oregon," Major Lillie explained as the boy returned to his seat. "They became ill and were abandoned by the train. Somehow David's father—just five or six years old at the time—managed to survive, and was found and adopted by the Comanche." He twirled the end of his mustache again. "Charles was the first Comanche warrior I ever met with blond hair and blue eyes. David's mother was the daughter of Little Ax, a Comanche war chief."

"Quite a heritage." Mother smiled.

The boy's eyes were almost defiant. He smiled back at her, but didn't say anything.

"Anyway," Major Lillie went on, "David here is the only one of my hands who's sharp enough to deal with those Omaha buyers. He's one of the best I've ever seen at riding and working stock—he even helps me with the bookkeeping. But those Omaha traders are slick as snakes. He lacks the experience to deal with them. I'll have to go myself."

Mother folded her arms and tilted her head to the side.

"What about the herd in Texas?"

Major Lillie shrugged. "First I heard of them was shortly before you contacted me. At that time they were some thirty miles from the town of San Antonio, and numbered close to fifty. The last I heard of them was from a man in the little settlement of Kerrville. They've moved farther up the Guadalupe River, and no one has seen them for weeks. At last count, he guessed their number at near thirty."

Mother sighed and again reached for the cigar.

"Sounds like half of them are already lost to us."

Major Lillie nodded. "Either lost to hunters and ranchers, or the herd split."

Mother started to take another puff from the cigar, then reconsidered and placed it in the ashtray.

"Well, Major Lillie, it does indeed sound like we have a problem. If you go after the ones in Omaha, you stand a good chance of losing the buffalo in Texas. The way the number has been cut on the Texan herd—if you don't go after them soon, they may all disappear."

Major Lillie traced his tongue across the right side of his mustache.

"I can't be in two places at once," he agreed. "I *know* where the buffalo are in Omaha. I know I can get them. I *don't* know where the herd is in Texas. It might take weeks to track them down. You know the old saying about a bird in the hand. Thus, my best bet is to go after the twenty head in Omaha and hope the bunch in Texas can hold out until we get time to find them later."

Everyone sat quietly for a long time. I glanced at the boy. Talltree, I thought. What a funny name. He looked toward me. Our eyes met for just an instant. Quickly I looked back at Mother.

I didn't like the look I saw on her face. There were wrinkles across her brow. A frown furrowed her soft, pretty face. I could tell she was buried deep in thought. That worried me, because when Mother thought really hard about something, it usually meant trouble.

Suddenly, she jerked and sat up very straight. A big smile curled her lips, and she reached for her cigar.

"I have a solution, Major Lillie," she announced confidently. "You go to Omaha and get the buffalo there. Mr. Talltree can take us to Texas to find the herd."

Everyone jumped, even me. I couldn't help noticing the startled look on the boy's face. Major Lillie held up his hands.

"Now, Mrs. Guthridge," he began, "I don't think David is mature enough to take the responsibility for you and your daughter on such a journey."

Mother shook her head. "I will take full responsibility. You yourself said that David was the best man you had with stock. I have seen firsthand his skill at riding and shooting a rifle. I also trust that his Indian upbringing has made him quite accomplished as a tracker. What better person to send looking for the buffalo herd in Texas?

"Finding the buffalo will be time consuming. While we search for them, you could finish your business in Omaha, then come join us and take them back to your ranch, where they would be safe."

It took a second for Major Lillie to close his mouth. He stroked his chin thoughtfully.

"Well . . . ah . . ." he stammered finally. "I don't know why it wouldn't work . . . and . . . ah . . . well, since you're so determined to make the trip . . . and . . ."

David stood up from his chair. He tugged at the black tie around his neck like it was a hangman's noose.

"Excuse me, sir. May I speak bluntly?"

Major Lillie looked at Mother. She nodded.

"I mean *very* bluntly," David said.

Mother nodded her approval again. So did Major Lillie.

David let go of his necktie and sat down.

"I'm not sure it's a good idea for me to take this lady and her daughter into the hill country of Texas. That was your idea, Major, not mine." He looked straight at me. "I mean, shoot—this little girl probably can't even ride a horse, and I'm not about to go off to Texas with—"

A puff of red smoke burst before my eyes. I took a huge drink of my lemonade, then slammed the glass down on the table so hard, I was surprised it didn't break. I didn't care, though.

Suddenly I was on my feet. I put my fists on my hips and glared at the boy.

"I'll have you know that I've been riding since I was five," I snarled. "That long-legged gray you were riding this afternoon looks good on flat ground, but if you were to try running him cross-country with jumps and trees, I could ride circles around you."

The boy pushed back his chair and stood again. I folded my arms. His chin jutted out. Tossing my hair to the side with a jerk of my head, I glared at him.

"And don't ever call me 'little girl' *again*. I'm fifteen. Besides," I huffed, "you hardly look old enough to be dry behind the ears yourself."

With two strides of those long legs David crossed the room and stood directly in front of me. "Excuse me. Perhaps the term *little girl* was incorrect."

He smiled.

His face was mildly handsome, but the ugly smile that he forced was more of a leer. It made him seem most unattractive.

"Perhaps the term *spoiled brat* would be more appropriate."

I leaned forward and tried to leer back at him. We were so close, our noses almost touched.

"Spoiled brat," I muttered. "Why, you crude, rude country bumpkin. If you think—"

"David!" Major Lillie shouted.

"Amanda!" Mother scolded from behind me, cutting me off.

Neither one of us blinked. Neither one of us moved. We stood so close I could smell the coffee on his breath.

"*David!*" Major Lillie barked again. The boy blinked first. He gave me one last hateful look, then returned to his chair. I waited until he'd moved away, then sat beside Mother on the couch.

David sat on the edge of his chair. He cleared his throat and squinted at me. "I'm sure you look quite prim and proper in your full skirt, sitting sidesaddle on some old plug back home. Out here, riding a horse is more than looks. Still, you seem so confident in your riding ability, why not put your money where your mouth is?"

"I shall!"

Instantly, I leaned toward Mother. "What does that mean?" I whispered from the side of my mouth, hoping no one would notice.

"He wants to make a wager. A bet," she whispered back.

Now that I knew what "put your money where your mouth is" meant, I smiled at him.

"How about a horse race?" I suggested, almost boasting. "How much would you like to wager?"

David smiled and rubbed his hands together.

"A horse race sounds fine. I'd hate to take your mother's money, though."

I detested the way he stretched out the word *mother*. I cocked my head to the side and leaned forward.

"Then what do you propose?"

He folded his arms and leaned way back in the chair. "Quite simply, if I win—you and your mother go home! Leave man's work to us men. If, on the other hand, you win . . ." he almost laughed ". . . I will gladly and graciously take you and your mother to search for the buffalo herd in Texas."

I glanced around the room. A pillar of smoke came from Colonel Stewart's cigar. Major Lillie looked rather sullen and irritated as he stared at his young cowhand.

"It's an unfair advantage, David," he said softly. "You know that you and Yankee have never lost a race."

David looked a little sheepish. Then he turned back

to me and smiled. "Very well. The brat doesn't have to win. I figure she won't even be within sight when I cross the finish line. Reckon that ought to be enough to put her in her place." He turned to me with that leering smile. "How about it? If it's a close race, I'll reconsider takin' you and your mom to Texas."

Mrs. Stewart's eyes met mine. She gave a quick shake of her head, as if trying to warn me of something. I looked at Mother. A little smile reassured me that her confidence in my ability was as great as my own. She hesitated only a moment and shrugged. "Why not?" she whispered.

I rose from the chair as gracefully as I could. I stood very straight and smoothed the front of my dress with my hands. Then I smiled, as hateful a smile as I could manage.

"You, Mr. Country Bumpkin, have a bet!"

CHAPTER 5

"Children should be seen and not heard."

When I was younger, Mother had told me that on more than one occasion. It was one of Grandmother's favorite sayings as well. I no longer thought of myself as a child. But after losing my temper last evening and challenging David Talltree to a horse race, I certainly felt like one.

It was bad enough that everybody at Fort Sill had heard about the race. What was worse, it seemed like all of Oklahoma Territory had been informed. There were soldiers with their blue uniforms, women in cotton dresses, and barefoot children. Three wagons with farmers and their families had arrived about eleven—with picnic baskets, no less. By noon, even some of the Indians from the reservation had come. A clump of about twenty or so, with bright-colored blankets, sat on the side of a hill nearly a quarter of a mile from the white spectators.

I knew that their only reason for being here was to laugh and make fun of the "little girl from San Francisco," the little girl who had spoken out of turn and who was about to make a total fool of herself.

It was one of those no-win situations. If I won the race, I'd have to go to Texas. Who in his right mind would ever want to go to Texas? If I lost, I could go home. But—*but*—that smart-mouthed, rude David Talltree would then have the satisfaction of having put me in my place.

No matter what I did, I couldn't get out of this mess. If only I'd kept my mouth shut. If only I'd thought about what I was saying before saying it. If only . . .

I rolled my eyes up toward the sky.

"You about ready, Miss Guthridge?"

The deep rumbling sound of Sergeant Sparks's voice startled me. I jumped and stepped back from the open stable door where I had been watching the crowd gather.

He stood beside the paint horse I had picked out from the herd this morning. White except for the brown blotches on his shoulder and hip, the paint was a tall, lanky animal—almost sixteen hands high. Sergeant Sparks was a huge man. He seemed to tower above my horse, making him look like one of the little Welsh ponies that pulled carriages up Nob Hill.

"Miss Guthridge? You ready to mount up?"

Sergeant Sparks ran a hand over his bald head. Even in the dark stable his bald dome seemed to shine.

Bravely I started toward him. I walked a couple of steps before my knees felt weak and my shoulders sagged. I glanced back at the crowd, then turned to the only friend I had.

"I don't stand a chance, do I, Sergeant Sparks?"

He led the paint to where I stood, slumped in the middle of the stable. His hand was so big it seemed to cover my whole back when he reached out to give me an understanding pat. I leaned my head against his shoulder and gave his arm a little hug. With Sergeant Sparks, I was safe to be the insecure child I felt like being at that moment.

Sergeant Sparks was the first person who had been *really* nice to me since I'd left home. He was in charge of the stables at Fort Sill. As such, he was to lay out the course for the race. He had also been assigned to come for me early this morning and help me pick out the horse I would ride.

He was always polite. He never once called me "little girl." Instead, he always addressed me as "Miss Guthridge." He had been most impressed by the three horses I had picked out earlier that morning. In fact, that's when I felt that we really started to become friends.

"You've only been here five minutes, Miss Guthridge," he'd said, "and you've managed to pick out the three best mounts we have on the whole post."

He had seemed quite proud of me.

We eliminated the tall, sleek black horse. Sergeant Sparks said he could probably keep up with David's gray on the flats, but he wasn't a jumper. The sorrel gelding was another good choice, but Sergeant Sparks said that he shied at noise. "If it's a close race and the crowd starts cheering when you get near the finish," he'd told me, "that sorrel is liable to jump out from under you and head off cross-country. Your best bet is the paint. The United States Cavalry doesn't use paint horses. This one was a colt that belonged to David's father. I fancied him, so I kept him even though I wasn't supposed to. He's not as fast as some, but he's a good jumper and quick in the trees. Besides, he's got more heart than any horse I've ever known."

Sergeant Sparks also told me that Mrs. Stewart had offered the use of her sidesaddle. "It's a jumping saddle," he assured me. "There's a down-curving horn under the regular side horn, so you can hook your left knee under."

I smiled at him. "Frankly, Sergeant Sparks, I prefer an English saddle."

Sergeant Sparks jerked. For an instant I thought I saw a touch of red sweep across his bald head.

I shrugged. "My instructor at the Riding Academy in San Francisco says that when the bicycle became popular in the early 1890s, wearing pants and riding astride a horse became acceptable for women," I explained. "I can ride both ways, but I think that with all the brush and all the jumps, I'd fare much better riding an English saddle."

Sergeant Sparks chuckled.

"Not only are you a good judge of horses, Miss Guthridge, but you also got pretty good sense when it comes to how to ride a race. Think you're gonna do right well."

Since the fort didn't have an English saddle, he had found me an artillery saddle, called a Grimsley. He had cut the cantle and pommel down to make it lighter. It was very close to what I was used to. Then Sergeant Sparks walked through the whole, entire race course with me. He showed me every jump and every twist and turn in the two-mile trail.

I glanced at the crowd outside, then turned to Sergeant Sparks with a sigh. "I'm going to make a complete fool of myself, aren't I, Sergeant Sparks?"

He knelt down on one knee. As big as he was, we were almost eye to eye.

Holding my arm gently with one hand, he reached into the pocket of his blue pants with the yellow stripe and pulled out a fistful of money.

"Sergeant Roark, over to Supply, is giving a hundred to one odds on David. I got thirty dollars here." He jiggled the money at me. "Little better than a month's wages. I'm bettin' every bit of it on you."

My mouth began to tremble.

"Oh, please don't. It wouldn't be right for you to lose that much—"

"Now, miss," he cut me off, patting my arm. "If I didn't think you could win, I wouldn't bet—not even at a thousand to one odds. I think you got a chance. A good chance. Just *do* what I told you."

With that, he got to his feet. Picking me up, as if I were no heavier than the feather pillow on my bed at home, he gently set me on the paint's back.

"You know what kind of money we're talking at a hundred to one odds?" He smiled, stuffing the money into his pocket. "When this race is over, I'm gonna be three thousand dollars richer. Shoot, Miss Guthridge, I could retire on money like that."

I took a deep breath and shook my head.

"I really wish you wouldn't . . ."

He held the paint's bridle and patted my arm with his free hand.

"You're a good judge of horses. You've walked this paint through every inch of the course—taken most of the jumps a couple of times on him. I've seen you ride. Them people down there ain't. You're good. You can win."

"But . . . but," I stammered as he started my horse toward the parade grounds.

"Ain't no buts about it, Miss Guthridge." Sergeant Sparks walked backward so he could face me. "Yankee, David's horse, is probably the best there is in the whole territory. David's probably one of the best riders. And he, along with most everybody else, figures you're just a little girl who don't know beans about horses or riding. I know better. I've watched you all morning."

With a jerk of his bald head, he motioned to where all the people stood. "David had a chance to come and take a look at the race course. He's so cocksure of himself, he didn't figure it was worth messing with. That's where we're gonna beat him. Now, you listen tight while we're walking to the starting line. I'll tell you how we're gonna run this race and how we'll beat that big-shot, loud-mouthed David Talltree."

Sergeant Sparks told me to hold my horse back until we got to the trees. Even if I had to pull on the reins, which the sergeant and I both doubted, I was not to even think about passing David's horse. Once in the trees, I was to let the paint go. "He's a better jumper and a lot quicker in the trees than Yankee," Sergeant Sparks said. "That's where you'll beat him. You'll have to be a hundred yards or so ahead when you come out of the trees and onto the parade grounds. But . . . if that one jump by the creek works like I think it will, and if you *do* what I told you to, you should be able to handle it."

We were almost to the crowd of people by the starting line. I pulled on the reins and made Sergeant Sparks and the paint stop.

"What jump? What do you mean, if it works like you think it will?"

Sergeant Sparks glanced over his shoulder, making sure no one was close enough to hear. He stood on his tiptoes and leaned near my ear.

"Remember that one spot where your horse refused the jump?"

I nodded, picturing the big log laid across the path at the edge of a small stream. The stream bank dropped away steeply on the other side of the log, and there was a low-hanging tree branch that stuck out across the path. I remembered taking the paint over that place two or three times to make sure he would jump and to make sure I knew where to duck so I wouldn't hit the limb.

Sergeant Sparks glanced around once more. "Horses hate to jump when they can't see where they're landing," he whispered. "Way I got it figured, David will get behind you once you're in the trees. That's gonna upset the boy, and he'll be working old Yankee hard as he can to pass you again."

He looked around one last time to make sure no one was listening to us. Then he tugged my arm. I leaned my ear so close it almost touched his lips.

"Once you and the paint clear the jump," he whispered, "here's what I want you to do. . . ."

The gray called Yankee reared. He spun around on his hind legs, his front hooves pawing the air. David, in a checkered calico shirt, sat very straight and proud. Yankee made a snorting sound. He landed, digging at the ground and ready to go.

I expected David to give me a sneer or at least an irritated look as he rode up. The young man didn't even glance in my direction. He totally ignored me.

Sergeant Sparks led my paint to the edge of the crowd, where Mother stood with a worried look on her face. I leaned down, and she kissed me on the cheek.

"I know you're a good rider, dear," she said, "but please be careful."

A young soldier came running up from the other direction and stood behind Sergeant Sparks. He waved a yellow cloth in his hand.

"Want my bandanna, little girl? Might keep you from choking on the dust from Yankee's heels."

He laughed, a loud, rude laugh. A group of young soldiers behind him burst into laughter too.

Sergeant Sparks's hand rested on the reins at the horse's neck. He removed it, and I saw his fist clench. Without looking back, he spun around to face the soldier.

Only when he turned, his elbow crashed into the young man's nose. The soldier flew backward, landing spread-eagled in the dust. Sergeant Sparks tried to look surprised.

"Sorry, son." He grinned. "Didn't see you standing that close."

He helped the boy up. Then he took the bandanna that the boy offered me and started dabbing at the blood that dripped from the kid's nose. His eyes seemed to sparkle and dance as he looked up at me.

"Get on out to the starting line, miss. You can do it. Just remember what I told you."

I smiled back at him and winked. Then slowly,

calmly, I moved the paint to the starting line, beside the gray.

People cheered and yelled. My heart stopped and chills raced up my back—not like chills usually do, but like a locomotive chugging along my spine.

I had been feeling better about the race. I felt almost good after Sergeant Sparks had told me what to do. In fact, when he told me about the jump, I had even laughed. Sergeant Sparks's bald head had turned a bright red. He had laughed too.

But now, standing in front of all these people and watching the gray's nostrils flare with the excitement of the race—now, I was scared.

I forced myself to swallow the big knot that crept into my throat. I held tight to the saddle. I checked the reins.

Colonel Stewart raised his revolver.

"On your mark."

I tightened my hold on the reins.

The colonel cocked the hammer.

"Get set."

Almost frantic, I looked at Sergeant Sparks. He smiled a warm, glowing smile, then winked at me.

I took a deep breath.

The shot exploded from Colonel Stewart's revolver.

"GO!"

CHAPTER 6

The race went exactly as Sergeant Sparks said it would. At the sound of the shot, David and Yankee leaped out in front of us. There *was* a cloud of dust, only it cleared quickly as the paint and I raced after them.

By the time we crossed the flat on the far side of the fort, rounded the stables, and raced toward the hill where the first flag stood, David was some twenty yards ahead.

My paint was fast and had great spirit. David stayed ahead of us, but he never gained any more than that twenty yards. We were keeping up with him.

Between the hill and the trees, there were a couple of small ravines. Yankee slowed before jumping each of them. My paint never broke stride. By the time we reached the edge of the trees, we had closed on the big gray.

Dodging and weaving, we gained on him steadily. I leaned forward, crouched low against the paint's neck. I was so close to him we were almost one. My cheek rested against his neck. Our breath came in short, quick gasps. His mane whipped and swirled in the wind, sometimes making it hard for me to see the trees and the little trail.

Finally we gained on Yankee's pounding hooves, and my paint's nose almost touched the gray's tail. But the little path was so narrow we couldn't pass. The trees were too close and thick for us to move up to the side. Grapevines and briars dangled from the oaks. More than once their spiny thorns caught my blouse and khaki riding skirt. I heard the material rip. I clung tighter to the paint's neck, urged him even closer.

My horse bumped into the back of the gray—once, then a second time. David glanced over his shoulder. He glared at me, and his angry blue eyes seemed to cut into me. I only smiled.

Ahead, there was a place where the path split and circled on both sides of a huge brush pile. It didn't matter which path David and Yankee picked—since I'd walked the trail with Sergeant Sparks, I knew they were both pretty much the same. Now was my big chance.

David took the left path. I kicked my paint hard. He surged forward, carrying me around the right side of the brush. On the other side of the dead trees I could hear Yankee popping and cracking through the small limbs. I kicked the paint again.

At the far side of the brush pile, the path came together again. From the corner of my eye, I could see David. We moved stride for stride. I was no longer behind him, but I wasn't ahead either. We were side by side as we charged toward where the two paths would meet.

I shoved the reins forward on the paint's neck and kicked him again. Then, holding tight to the saddle, I braced for the crash that I knew was coming.

At the last second David pulled up. His gray bumped into the back of my paint. We stumbled, but the paint kept his feet. My leg bumped against a small tree on the side of the path. I winced at the sharp pain, but kept going.

We were ahead at last.

There were five or six jumps along the path: tree limbs, two white-cross fences, and some hedges that had been planted to challenge the soldiers who used this trail to practice their riding skills. With each jump David and Yankee fell a bit more behind. But as we neared the far edge of the trees and the last jump, they were no more than twenty yards or so away from us.

I remembered Sergeant Sparks's words: "You'll have to be a hundred yards or so ahead when you come out of the trees and onto the parade grounds. . . . Here's what I want you to do. . . ."

My paint slowed as we got closer to the big log that stretched across the path. His ears perked forward. I let him slow down, let him remember how we had practiced this very jump three times earlier that morning.

He took the jump.

I kept my cheek against his neck. My fingernails dug into the leather saddle as I braced for the downhill landing. Despite every instinct that made me want to lean back, I stayed down on his neck until we cleared the low-hanging limb and raced up the creek bank on the far side.

At the crest of the bank, I pulled the paint to a stop. I looked back and did *exactly* what Sergeant Sparks had told me to do.

"Hurry up, little boy!" I screamed at the top of my lungs. "You ride like an old squaw!"

David was almost to the log. His fury at my words curled his lip to a sneer. He kicked the gray so hard in the sides, it looked like he might have knocked the air from the magnificent animal. Only Yankee was a better horse than Sergeant Sparks or I had given him credit for.

He didn't refuse the jump.

He didn't slide to a stop and send David flying over his neck and head as we had imagined. Instead, he obeyed the boy's command. He jumped.

Suddenly I realized what Sergeant Sparks had meant when he said, "Yankee will probably stop and send David flying over his head. But if he don't—we still got 'em anyway."

Yankee came flying over the log. All four legs were outstretched and locked for the downhill landing.

David did what any rider would do when taking a downhill jump. He braced his hand against the horse's neck and leaned back.

Yankee made the jump.

David didn't.

The low-hanging tree limb that dangled over the path hit him square in the chest.

There was a loud cracking sound—the sound of wood breaking. Then came a startled:

"Whoompf!"

Then a splash.

For a second I thought the boy was dead. He'd hit the tree limb with such force, it snapped clean. He and the limb landed, flat, in the bottom of the creek. A huge wall of water and mud shot up.

I strained my eyes, trying to see him. I couldn't. Right then I felt almost guilty for what Sergeant Sparks and I had done. What if David were really injured? What if . . .

The water and mud cleared. With the tree limb cradled in his arms, David sat up. His eyes were crossed. For a second, they kind of rolled around in his head before they came to focus on me.

And . . . when I saw that look in his eyes. . . .

Suddenly I was no longer worried whether I'd hurt him. I was no longer worried whether I would win the race or not.

Suddenly—when I saw his eyes—I had this strange feeling that if he ever got up from the bottom of that creek and got his hands on me . . .

I yanked the paint's head around and spun him toward the edge of the trees. Behind me I could hear the boy struggling to his feet. I heard him call for his horse.

I never rode so hard in my whole life. I wasn't riding to win a race—not now. Now, I was riding for my very life.

That half-crazed Comanche was going to kill me.

My only chance was to get to Mother and Sergeant Sparks before he caught me.

I was afraid to look back, but I couldn't help myself. He and the gray broke from the trees behind me. They were a good hundred yards or so away. Yankee's feet gobbled up the ground in huge strides. I could hear the thunderous pounding of the horse's mighty hooves.

A little squeal just sort of popped out of my throat. I kicked the paint harder.

In the distance I could hear the people cheering and yelling. I held the reins on either side of the paint's neck. The wind barely touched me as I leaned forward and kicked him again and again and again.

As I drew nearer to the huge crowd at the finish line, their cheers and yells rose like a solid wall of noise. It was deafening. I didn't see the people. I didn't listen to their cheers. My eyes focused on the finish line.

There was safety there. There was Mother and there was the sergeant who would protect me. There was . . .

There was David!

Just a few yards from the finish line, he and the big gray stallion drew alongside us. And as we crossed the line, my paint's nose was even with the gray's shoulder.

David won.

CHAPTER 7

The instant I crossed the finish line, I pulled the paint to a stop and leaped off. Leading him with the reins, I charged through the crowd, desperately trying to find Mother and Sergeant Sparks.

It took forever to reach them. People were cheering and laughing and clapping. They would reach out and pat me on the back or slap me on the shoulder. I practically had to fight my way through them.

At last, I spotted the huge man in the blue uniform. He came charging toward me. His thundering laugh drowned out all the other sounds. His enormous hands reached out and clamped about my sides, and he lifted me straight up in the air.

"Best race I ever seen in my life!" he roared. "You come a-one of beatin' 'em. Best race I ever seen!"

He hugged me against his chest so hard my eyes nearly popped out. I wrapped my arms around his thick neck, enjoying his happiness and feeling the safety of being with him. His laughter rumbled in my ears, and he hugged me even tighter.

Beside us I could see Mother. She smiled, but there was worry in her eyes. She reached up and patted my arm.

"Are you all right, dear?" she asked, frowning at the rips where the thick brush had torn my riding skirt. "You're not hurt, are you?"

I smiled down at her. "I'm fine."

Sergeant Sparks put me down. People kept coming up to say things, to pat me on the shoulder. Others wanted to shake my hand or pet the paint horse.

For the life of me, I couldn't understand it.

Finally Sergeant Sparks roared at everybody to step back and let my horse and me have some air. When the excitement settled, I looked up and tugged at the sleeve of his blue uniform.

"I lost," I said. "Why is everybody so excited?"

With a jerk of his bald head, he motioned to the other side of the crowd. I could see a group of young soldiers. They were clumped about the boy and the big gray. As they moved about, congratulating him on his victory, I could see David.

He was covered with mud from the creek. It had dried and matted his brown hair. A big scratch ran from the corner of his mouth up to his left ear. There were little cuts and scratches all across his bare chest

and arms from the tree limb that knocked him from
Yankee's back.

"Boy looks like he's been in a fight with a bobcat."
Sergeant Sparks chuckled. "You gave him one heck of
a race, Miss Guthridge. Darned near beat him."

I shrugged.

"So?"

Sergeant Sparks smiled down at me.

"So," he repeated. "Ain't nobody ever done that
before. David lived on the reservation with his folks
until they died and Major Lillie sort of adopted him.
Everybody round these parts knows him and Yankee." He made a sweeping motion with his long
arm. "Most every soldier on this post and half the
braves on the Indian reservation—most anybody
who fancies himself a good rider—has challenged
David to some kind of race. Ain't never been beat—
not once."

He looked down and gently cupped my face between his big hands.

"But you—you, young Miss Amanda Guthridge—
you come closer than anybody ever has to takin' him
down a notch or two."

His barrel chest seemed to puff out with pride. He
laughed then, a deep, rumbling laugh.

His smile seemed to stretch from ear to ear. He
laughed so hard his bald head turned a bright shade of
red. Finally he put a big hand on my shoulder.

"Your horse has worked up a pretty good lather.
Let's get out of this crowd and go wipe him down."

*   *   *

Colonel Stewart invited us to join him and his wife
at their home for dinner. But since Sergeant Sparks
had asked Mother and me first, they did not appear
the least insulted that we chose to eat with him.

I felt great. Even though I lost the race, I had ridden well. I came close to beating David. That made
me feel good.

Sergeant Sparks liked me, and he was proud of me.
That made me feel good too.

The only thing that worried me was the thought that
David said he might reconsider if it was a close race,
but surely his pride wouldn't let him. With luck, I
could be back in my room on Nob Hill within the
week.

Sergeant Sparks came for Mother and me about six
o'clock. We rode in a small carriage to a long, narrow
building just on the far side of the fort. He tied the
horse and carriage to a hitching rail out front and
helped us down. A line of men stood waiting outside
the door. As we approached, they removed their blue
hats and stepped out of our way.

Inside, there were three rows of tables and chairs.
At the far end of these rows was a kitchen. The food
smelled wonderful. I guess riding a race had given me
more of an appetite than I'd imagined.

The wooden tables were bare, except for one at the

far end, near the kitchen. It was covered with a white tablecloth and fine dishes. Some men with yellow stripes on the arms of their uniforms like Sergeant Sparks's stood waiting for us. They remained standing until Mother and I were seated, then joined us at the table. Sergeant Sparks introduced each to us. After that a man with a white apron scurried from the kitchen and served our meal.

The soldiers came from the line near our table with their food on small tin platters. They sat at the other tables and talked softly while they ate.

The food, though not as fancy as the meal Mrs. Stewart had fixed, was excellent. Of course, the fact that I was so hungry didn't hurt the taste of chicken, mashed potatoes, and green beans either.

We were almost finished eating when I noticed a sudden hush fall over the soldiers around us.

The hush turned to an ominous silence, a silence that seemed to sweep across the mess hall like some giant wave rolling across the ocean.

I turned. There, at the open doorway to the mess hall, were David Talltree and Major Lillie.

All eyes turned toward them as they closed the door and started toward our table. Straight and stiff as one of the soldiers standing at attention, David moved to the end of our table. He stopped and removed his cowboy hat.

I couldn't help but notice how he sort of crunched it in his fist instead of sweeping it gently from his head. Major Lillie took his hat off too.

There must have been well over a hundred soldiers in the mess hall. Not a sound came from any of them, not so much as a word, a tinkle of forks, or a gulping of water. The whole room seemed to quake with the silence.

"Mrs. Guthridge?" David said and nodded politely to Mother. "Miss Guthridge." He nodded to me. "It is my sincere hope that neither of you were offended by any remark I might have made last night concerning Miss Guthridge's riding ability. If you were, I truly apologize."

Mother nodded back to him. "No offense was taken, Mr. Talltree."

He looked at me, only I didn't nod at him or say anything. I just folded my arms and glared.

David cleared his throat. There was almost a pained look on his face when he spoke again.

"You are a very good rider, Miss Guthridge."

I only stared at him.

"I was most impressed by your performance during the race this afternoon, and . . ."

He stopped. His eyes kind of shot up toward the sky, as if looking for God or the Great Spirit to help him. He started to turn around. Only, I saw Major Lillie jab him in the back of the ribs with his thumb.

". . . And, David?" Major Lillie prompted.

David took a deep breath. He wouldn't look at me.

"And?" Major Lillie gouged him with his thumb once more.

"And," David snapped, his eyes almost boring a hole in the floor beside me, "I would be most honored to accompany the two of you on a search for the buffalo herd in Texas."

My mouth fell open. Before I could speak, he spun around and crushed his hat down so hard on his head, it was almost flat. He stormed halfway across the mess hall before Sergeant Sparks stood and called after him.

"David!" he roared.

The boy stopped, but he didn't turn around.

"Why don't you come join us for dinner? The cook's prepared a special meal for you."

Slowly, an inch at a time, the boy turned around. Sergeant Sparks's smile seemed to jerk and bounce and dance across his face. He pointed a thumb toward the kitchen. The soldier in the white apron reached down behind the counter. He straightened and held up something in his right hand. A big bird—black as the night sky—dangled from one leg.

A roar of laughter shook the mess hall. Soldiers pounded the tables with their fists. One man fell out of his chair. Sergeant Sparks doubled over, holding his stomach. Even Major Lillie laughed.

I leaned over. "What is it, Mother?" I whispered in her ear.

"A crow."

I frowned, barely able to hear above the roaring laughter.

"I don't get it," I whispered. "What's so funny?"

Mother leaned very close to my ear so I could hear above the noise.

"You know back home when somebody says something, then wishes he hadn't said it?" she explained. "We have an expression for it. You know, we say 'somebody put his foot in his mouth.' "

I nodded.

"So?"

Mother smiled. "Out here, the expression is 'eating crow.' In other words, David bragged about your not being able to ride, and you almost beat him. So they fixed him crow for supper."

A smile tugged at my lips. David started to say something. Instead, he reached up with both hands and pulled his hat down, harder, on his head. He had it so far down that the tops of his ears flattened and stuck out under the brim.

The roaring laughter followed him out the door and into the darkness.

To me it wasn't that funny. In fact, when I thought about what David had said, my smile quickly disappeared altogether.

"I would be most honored to accompany the two of you on a search for the buffalo herd in Texas." His words seemed to drum in my memory much, much louder than the laughter.

Suddenly I didn't feel so good anymore.

Not only had I lost the race, I had managed to lose it so well that now I still had to go to Texas.

If I'd only known, I would have ridden backward. I

would have fallen off the paint and cried like a little baby.

Things just weren't working out like they were supposed to.

The lighthearted, happy feeling I had had earlier was gone. Now—now, I felt totally rotten.

(

CHAPTER 8

The next morning, as we looked at a map of the United States and listened to Major Lillie in Colonel Stewart's office, I didn't feel quite so bad.

I guess I had a vision of the Oklahoma Territory, and especially Texas, as a vast, empty wilderness. When we had reached the tiny town of Rush Springs, which was the end of the railroad line, I really felt that it was *the end of the line*.

I had pictured us traveling in a freight wagon or on horseback for weeks, even months, to get to the place in Texas called Kerrville where the buffalo had last been seen. It would take even longer to drive them back to Pawnee in the Oklahoma Territory.

What made me smile was that it wasn't going to be like that at all. According to the map, there were railroad lines all over the place.

"Think our best bet," Major Lillie said, pointing at the map, "is for y'all to take the Rock Island from Rush Springs back up to El Reno. We'll have to switch trains and go east to connect with the Katy. There I'll head north to Omaha and y'all will go on down to San Antonio. I've already sent a message for three of my top hands to meet us at El Reno tomorrow."

David moved up beside him. "Charlie, Les, and . . ." he asked.

"And Pepper," the major answered. Turning to Mother, he said, "Won't hurt to have a few extra hands with you. They're good men—honest and trustworthy."

Mother nodded her agreement. Then she frowned. "But Major Lillie, are six of us going to be enough to herd the buffalo back to your ranch?"

Major Lillie sort of laughed. David smiled at Mother. When his eyes met mine, the corners of his mouth drooped.

"You don't herd buffalo, ma'am," he said flatly.

Mother gave a little jerk. "But . . . but . . ." she stammered.

"David's right," Major Lillie assured her. "Buffalo aren't like cattle, Mrs. Guthridge. You don't round them up and herd them fifteen, twenty miles a day. They're wild animals. Rider and horse comes up on them, they either stampede or turn and fight."

"Usually stampede," David jumped in. "They take off like lightning—most times, headed where you *don't* want the darned things to go. Then you got to race alongside them, either trying to turn 'em or hoping they don't turn on you."

Mother blinked. She tried to make herself look calm, but I could tell she was confused.

"If we can't herd them or drive them like cattle"—Mother tilted her head to the side—"then how will we get them back to your ranch?"

"Railroad," Major Lillie said, tapping the end of his stick on the map. "In San Antonio or Kerrville we'll have to hire on extra hands, buy lumber, and arrange for wagons and drivers. Once you find the herd, David will take a good hard look at the lay of the land and figure where they'll run once they get started. Then you have to build a solid, open-mouth corral and try to chase the herd into it. When you get that done, you crate 'em up and haul them back on the wagons to the nearest railhead. Load them on stock cars and run them back up to the ranch at Pawnee."

Mother shook her head. Weakly, she felt for the chair behind her and sank into it.

"It all sounds so quick and easy." She sort of breathed the words instead of saying them. Then a meek smile came to her face. "I'm sorry," she confessed. "I guess I've read too many stories about the early cattle drives. I had this romantic vision of herding the buffalo to the Oklahoma Territory. You know, days spent riding the range and nights sleeping under the starry sky."

"I'm sorry, Mrs. Guthridge," Major Lillie apologized. "But there ain't nothin' romantic about a cattle drive."

He cleared his throat with a serious look on his face and pulled up a chair and sat down in front of Mother. "I *am* sorry," he said again. "So many people from the East, or out in California, have the same vision about cattle drives and Texas. Things aren't like that anymore. Civilization has finally reached us, even out here on the prairie.

"Cattle drives are a thing of the past. They were romanticized by the dime novels and by the newspapers. In reality they were nothing but months of hard, dirty work.

"You will have the opportunity to spend nights under the starry sky, as you put it. It will take time to find the herd and time for the men to build the corral."

He left his chair for a moment and drew our attention back to the map. "San Antonio has rail service. There are even a few of those automobile things running up and down the streets. There's a spur line planned for Kerrville, but it's not under construction yet."

He traced a big circle on the map with his finger.

"This area on the Guadalupe River is in the hill country. There are no hotels and very few houses. Fact, there ain't much of anything except deer, turkey, bobcat, and mountain lion. The only towns around"—he jabbed a finger at the paper—"Kerrville, Uvalde, Eldorado. They're little towns, but they're still as wild and rough as any Texas town you might have read about in your dime novels. You'd all do well to stay away from them as much as possible." Major

Lillie glanced over his shoulder, making sure David was listening. He took a deep breath. He sat down again in the chair in front of Mother. He took her hand and looked her straight in the eye.

"It *is* wild country, Mrs. Guthridge. And anytime you work with buffalo, you're taking your life in your hands. It's hard, dangerous, dirty work. There is nothing adventurous or romantic about it. Now, if you've changed your mind . . . if you've decided not to go. . . ."

He stopped, giving Mother a moment to think over what he had said.

I held my breath and waited.

Finally Mother sighed. She smiled at Major Lillie. "My imagination had painted this beautiful picture of driving the buffalo across the prairie. It was a foolish and immature dream. But I still want to be a part of helping to save the buffalo. I want to actually be there to help. It is a cause that warrants much more than joining an organization or simply sending money to finance the endeavor. I have to be a part of it. Why . . ." Her voice kind of trailed off. She shrugged. "Why, I'm not quite sure. I only know that I can't stay here or go back home and wait."

She patted Major Lillie's hand. With as much grace and calm as she could muster, Mother stood up from her chair and held her shoulders back.

"Amanda and I will go with David and try to help. If we get in the way, we'll step aside and let him do what has to be done. But . . . I have to be there."

I quit holding my breath. The air whooshed out of me like the wind blowing from a busted balloon.

Major Lillie nodded.

David shrugged.

I pouted.

Then . . . then, I felt a tiny smile tug at the corners of my mouth. I was still stuck with going to Texas. But maybe it wouldn't be as bad as I thought. I had had much the same vision as Mother. Only to me there was nothing beautiful or romantic about it. To me it had seemed nothing but hard, dirty work and time away from my friends and my home and from Philip.

Now, instead of being stuck for months and months we were talking about a week or so. We would ride a train to San Antonio, stay in a nice hotel while David looked for men to help build a corral, round up the buffalo, and start back home.

I felt my little smile grow. Soon I'd be back in San Francisco, back in my own house, back in my own little bed with the goose-down quilt. I could hardly wait to start on our trip. The sooner we got started, the sooner I could get home.

CHAPTER 9

Most of our stay in San Antonio was at a fine hotel. While David and the other three men found wagons, drivers, and men who would go along and work on building the corral, Mother and I shopped in the rows of big stone buildings. The streets of San Antonio, though not paved with brick, were wide and packed tight. There was very little dust. We didn't see any of the automobiles that Major Lillie had mentioned. I was a bit disappointed. Father said they were nothing more than playthings for the rich, but I was still fascinated with them, and wished I could have seen some. There was also a theater, although there was no play going on during the short time we were there.

We stored our baggage at the train depot. David had said that there would be no room for "all that stuff" once we started our own search for the buffalo.

At first, I had the feeling that he was doing nothing more than trying to make the trip uncomfortable for us. But when we left San Antonio on horseback with only one packhorse to carry all our supplies, I realized that he was not being disagreeable.

The man called Pepper—I guess because he had white hair with only a few flecks of black sprinkled in it—stayed behind to make sure the wagons, drivers, and sixteen workers David had hired would follow us to Kerrville in a couple of days.

It was some seventy-eight miles from San Antonio to the little settlement of Kerrville. David had brought his horse, Yankee, in a stock car on the train. I'd brought the paint. He was a gift from both Colonel Stewart and Sergeant Sparks. Sergeant Sparks's bald head had turned red when I told him I would name the horse Sarge.

Though accustomed to riding, I was a bit stiff. We were outfitted with what my riding instructor called a double-rigged or rim-fire saddle, because it had two cinches. They were supposedly quite common on the Texas cattle drives, but I was not used to the hard seat or the long fenders and stirrups.

We spent one night camping along the trail. Les, a tall, slender man with rather plain features, built a small fire. He didn't talk much, but when he did, he was very polite. David helped gather wood and visited with Charlie.

Charlie was a Mexican with slick black hair and a long mustache. He was our cook. That first night he prepared cornbread and what he called "chili." It was a mixture of beans and meat. I ate very little, as it was much too spicy for my taste. I did try to act like I enjoyed it, though, because Charlie seemed to be a very nice man and was proud of the meal he had prepared.

Mother was thrilled by how quiet it was in the wilderness and how beautiful the night stars looked. I kept worrying about bugs or snakes crawling in the bedroll with me. I tossed and turned and barely slept all night. Little pesky mosquitoes hummed and buzzed about my head, and I must have spent half the night slapping at them.

Just before dawn I woke up. I felt uncomfortable and needed, desperately, to relieve myself. I hated to wake Mother, but finally I had to. Quietly she got the big thick Sears, Roebuck catalogue from the pack by the fire. Then she led me to a small clump of bushes a ways from the camp so I could take care of my business.

It was a bit embarrassing to have Mother take me, but it was hard to know what animals lurked nearby in the dark.

The mosquitoes kept buzzing around us. "Remind me to pick up some vanilla tomorrow, when we get to Kerrville," Mother whispered from the other side of the bushes.

For breakfast Charlie fixed scrambled eggs and ham. They were much better than the chili. David must have noticed how I gobbled them down. Only as soon as I saw him watching me, he quickly turned to Mother.

"Best enjoy your meal, Mrs. Guthridge," he said. "We should reach Kerrville by tonight. When we leave there in the morning, we'll have to pack light. Only jerky, flour, salt, sugar, lard, cornmeal, and beans, unless we can find game along the trail. This and the meals tonight and tomorrow morning will probably be the last time you get to enjoy 'real' food for quite a while."

There was a small hotel at Kerrville. Mother and I did not stay there. It only had one private room, which was already taken. The rest consisted of what was called a Common, a large open area with about ten to twelve beds. It was designed for the cattlemen or travelers who passed through the little town. But sleeping in a Common was no place for women. So, instead of the hotel, we stayed the night at Mrs. Pipton's boarding house at the edge of town.

She was a sweet gray-haired lady of sixty or so. Originally from Boston, she had married a Texas rancher and raised eight children in a large, two-story home. When her husband died and all her children married and moved away, she turned her home into a boarding house.

David came to the front door as we were finishing breakfast. He took off his hat and followed Mrs. Pipton to the dining room. There were two rolled-up blankets under his left arm. The boy wouldn't look at me, only at Mother.

"We'll be leaving soon." He laid the blankets on the floor beside Mother's chair. "I've made you a couple of bedrolls. You can put a change of clothes inside them, but that's all we'll have room to take."

My eyes flashed.

"How long are we going to be gone?" I asked.

He answered Mother instead of me. "At least a week."

"One change of clothes?" I yelped. "No hairbrush? No toiletries? I have to have at least five split riding skirts for a whole week. I just simply cannot—"

"One change of clothes," he snarled, glaring at me with those dark blue eyes. Then he whirled to look at Mother. "I'm sorry, ma'am, but that's all we got room for. The packhorse is already loaded down. Figured you and your daughter would need a tent. Rest of it's cookin' things and food stuff. Ain't no room for nothin' more. You'll have to carry your bedrolls on the back of your horses."

"Do we even get to take a bar of soap?" I huffed.

"We have two bars of lye soap already packed," he told Mother.

I slammed my fork down on my plate and sprang to my feet.

"Would you at least look at me when I speak to you?" I snapped. "Just because I almost beat you in that stupid race—well, it doesn't mean I'm going to hurt you if you look at me."

David stuffed his hat back on top of his head. Ever so slowly, he turned to face me.

"Why don't you stay here?" he mumbled, almost too softly for me to hear. "Maybe the school's got a nursery where you could stay while we're gone."

For an instant, I wished I were a man. I wanted to punch him, square in the nose.

Instead, I forced a big, broad smile to my face. It was a silly smile. I exaggerated it even more as his eyes bore into me like knives. He bit down so hard on his bottom lip that it turned white.

"Quit pestering the young man," Mother scolded after he stormed outside to wait with the horses.

"I can't stand him," I snapped back at her. "He's still mad about me almost beating him in that silly race. If we're going to be stuck with him for another week or longer, the least he could do is show enough respect to look at me when I speak."

"Now, Amanda," Mother soothed. "He beat you, but you came so close to winning that race, it *did* bruise his pride. It takes most men a little time to get over such things. Just don't bother him. Leave him alone, and I'm sure he'll come around soon and be more friendly."

"I don't care whether he's friendly or not!" I marched over and snatched one of the bedrolls from the floor. "He can drop dead, for all I care." Then I stomped off toward our room.

I picked up two split-skirt riding outfits, three silk blouses, three pairs of stockings and embroidered flannel drawers, and my hairbrush. Frowning, I laid them out on the bedroll. Even before I tried to roll it back up, I saw there would be no room for my bust pads or my hip bustle. I took the end of the blanket and began twisting. Even with as little as I had, it seemed impossible.

Suddenly there was a knock at the door. Mother opened it. Mrs. Pipton stood there with a pile of blue denim cradled in her arms. She smiled.

"My children left a bunch of Levis around the house when they married or went off to school. Figured you two could use them."

Mother's eyes sprang wide. "Levis? Those are men's pants."

Mrs. Pipton shrugged.

"Well . . . maybe they're considered men's pants in San Francisco or back East. Out here, women wear the things. Besides, they're easier to bedroll than those thick, duck riding skirts. They'll hold up to the brush better than a skirt, and they're a lot more comfortable."

Mother shook her head.

"Thank you, Mrs. Pipton. But we simply couldn't. It wouldn't be proper."

Mrs. Pipton tossed the bundle of denim onto the bed. "Mrs. Guthridge." She spoke softly. "This is Texas. Women are a mite more independent out here. We don't worry as much about what's proper as we do about what works. It's commonplace for women to wear Levis, especially for traveling on the trail. Besides, you and your daughter are riding into some pretty rough country. Chances are, you won't see another rider all the time you're out. Then again . . ."

She glanced at me. When she turned back to Mother, she pulled her gold-rimmed spectacles down on the tip of her nose.

"Were it me traveling with one of my daughters when she was Amanda's age, and were we to run onto a pack of ruffians, I'd just as soon they mistook us for men. At least from a distance."

Mother frowned. She pinched her bottom lip between her thumb and finger, thinking.

"Well . . ."

"Try 'em on, honey." Mrs. Pipton chuckled as she grabbed a pair of the Levis from the bed and tossed them to her. "They ain't half bad."

Mother hesitated, but for only a moment. Then both of us began trying on the pants. We giggled and laughed as we pulled on one pair after another. The pants were low waisted. They felt loose around my middle, but quite snug around my hips. Mrs. Pipton said they were stiff as cardboard and the indigo blue dye came off on everything when they were new. She said these were "broken in," and I was amazed at how soft and comfortable the cloth felt.

I was also a bit surprised at how wearing "men's pants" made me feel. My cheeks were a bright red when I looked at my reflection in the mirror. I felt just a bit wicked—naughty. The pants were tight around my hips and the slim, tapering legs made my own legs seem even longer.

Mrs. Pipton suggested that we leave our silk blouses

behind and wear something cotton or flannel. She also told us the sunbonnets and kid-and-cloth shoes wouldn't work well on the trail either.

"Make them boys who are riding with you stop by Carlin's Mercantile on the way out of town. Get yourself a Western hat and some calfskin boots. You'll be a lot better off."

When Mother and I came out the front door dressed in Levis and cotton blouses, David was sitting on his horse. He looked a bit bored. But the instant he saw us, he blinked and stiffened. For an instant he seemed surprised, but not as shocked as I had hoped he'd be. Then he got that mad, serious look on his face.

That's what made me smile. I smiled all the way through the little town of Kerrville. I smiled when we stopped at the mercantile store in town to buy vanilla for the mosquitoes and to get Mother and me hats and calfskin Western boots. I smiled when we crossed the little creek outside of town. I smiled every time David so much as acted like he might look in my direction.

I smiled until my jaws hurt and my mouth was so dry that my lips started sticking to my teeth.

CHAPTER 10

By the next morning, I couldn't even think about smiling.

My jaws hurt. I was tired. I felt dirty. I itched. I smelled bad. And I had indigestion.

Life on the trail simply wasn't that much fun.

First of all, my jaws hurt from all the "smiling" I had done yesterday. I guess it was what I deserved for being so unbending. I hadn't slept well. With the flap closed on our little tent, it was too hot to sleep. With it open, the mosquitoes swept in by the thousands. I didn't have many bites—the vanilla Mother wiped on my face, neck, and hands seemed to keep them from biting—but it didn't keep them from buzzing and humming around me all night. That kept me awake. I felt dirty and I smelled bad because we had spent all day riding and there was no place to take a bath. And although the cornbread and beans Charlie served for supper last night had been very good, they had given me a terrible case of indigestion.

The worst problem was my teeth. Of all things, I'd forgotten my toothbrush! I traced my tongue over my front teeth. They felt grungy and dirty—almost slimy. I had always been so proud of my teeth. Now I felt ashamed to so much as open my mouth to speak, much less smile.

Charlie fixed pancakes for breakfast. He called them flapjacks, but they were really pancakes. He made syrup for them by boiling water and adding sugar to it. They were quite good, but I didn't eat much. My stomach already felt like it was going to explode, and the flapjacks were filling.

Besides, I couldn't quit thinking about my teeth. I moped and didn't say a word to anyone the whole day. When Mother would ask me something, I would either nod or shake my head.

We rode on the flat above the Guadalupe River. On occasion we would drop down to the riverbank, because the thickets above became so dense with thorns and briars and twisted limbs that our horses couldn't get through.

The Guadalupe was one of the prettiest rivers I had seen since leaving the Rocky Mountains. Most of the streams and rivers in the prairie were brown. Some in the Oklahoma and Indian Territories had seemed almost red. The Guadalupe had a turquoise tint to it. It was a blue-green color where the river widened out and ran slow. In the narrows the water would come rushing together to form rapids. It gurgled and bubbled over the rocks, where it was almost as clear as the little glass angel on my trinket shelf back home.

Enormous trees lined the banks. They were taller than some of the masts I had seen on the big sailing ships in the harbor in New York, where I'd been once with Mother to visit friends. The trunks, especially at the base where they spread reaching for the water, were as big around as two or three horses standing side by side. Tremendous limbs hung over us and out over the river. The shade was cool. But the enormous trees with huge limbs had the teeniest leaves I had ever seen. Once when I passed under a low-hanging branch, I pulled off a little sprig. The leaves were no longer than an eyelash and not much wider than the thickness of my thumbnail. They looked a little like pine needles, only I could tell they weren't.

Charlie and the packhorse broke trail for us. I followed them, and Mother brought up the rear. She was not as accustomed to riding as I was, and I worried about her. David and Les were always far ahead. They would circle back, every now and then, to tell Mother and Charlie that there were still no signs of buffalo.

I nudged Sarge in the ribs. My paint stepped up beside Charlie's horse.

"What kind of tree is this?" I asked, covering my mouth with my hand so he wouldn't see my dingy teeth.

Charlie glanced over his shoulder to see where I was pointing with my other hand.

"Bald cypress," he answered. "Find a lot of 'em in the swamps or along the rivers, down here in lower Texas."

Still hiding my dingy teeth I asked, "Are they a kind of pine or evergreen?"

Charlie shrugged.

"Don't know. Leaves fall off ever' winter, though. They're just a pesky old swamp tree, I reckon."

At noon we stopped for about thirty minutes. We ate the stuff Charlie called jerky. It was dried beef he had smoked earlier over an open fire. It was cut in little thin strips and was about as tough as the sole of my boots. I ate some anyway. We let the horses rest while we stretched. My back and bottom were sore from all the riding. It felt good to walk around a bit.

I could tell Mother was uncomfortable too. She didn't complain, though.

Charlie warned us not to go near the river because of snakes. He also told us to watch out near clumps of dead tree limbs.

After resting a bit, we rode on.

About an hour before dark David appeared on the far bank of the river. He called to Charlie, then rode his horse into the water. Charlie pulled his horse to a stop. I saw him take his rifle from the leather holster on the side of his saddle.

David met us at a very wide part of the river. He stayed in his saddle until Yankee's feet no longer touched the bottom. Then he slipped off the animal's right side and held on to the saddle horn while his long-legged gray swam. As soon as Yankee touched mud on our side, David slid back into the saddle and rode up to meet us.

"Found some buffalo chips and about six carcasses."

Charlie shoved his rifle back into the holster.

"How old?"

David shrugged. "Couple of months. Maybe more." He slipped from his saddle, and leaning against his horse, pulled off his boot. "Found 'em about three miles up the river." He poured the water from his boot, put it on, and took off the other. "Good camping spot about a mile ahead. Figure we'll stay there the night and start again early in the morning."

When he was finished emptying the water from his other boot, he jumped back on Yankee.

We followed David to the place he'd found to camp. It was a little flat spot not far from the river. Surrounded by tall cypress trees, the grass was short and green. David left us, telling Charlie that he'd seen some turkey not far from here and would try to bring one bird back for supper. We unsaddled Sarge and the other horses, then helped Charlie unload the packhorse.

At the edge of the little clearing closest to the river, Charlie used the heel of his boot to scrape out a place in the dirt. Mother and I helped him pile rocks in a circle around the bare spot. Then we gathered dead, dry wood for a fire.

I sat down not far from the little fire that Charlie started. I pulled off my boots and rubbed my sore feet. Mother sat next to me and did the same.

It wasn't long before Les rode in. He hadn't seen any sign of buffalo at all. While he unsaddled his horse, Mother asked Charlie if we could bathe. He brought us a bar of brown soap and two small towels from one of the packs to use as washcloths.

"Watch for snakes," he warned as we headed toward the river.

Taking our blankets to use as towels, we went downstream—opposite the direction in which David had ridden off and far enough from our camp so we wouldn't be seen. Mother found a little sandy spot on the bank. It was surrounded by a clump of small willow trees that further sheltered us from the view of anyone at camp.

There we undressed and, watching for snakes as Charlie had told us to, slipped into the river.

It felt *wonderful!* We swam around for a while, gliding through the water and enjoying the cool, clean feel of it. Then Mother handed me the soap. It didn't smell as nice as my perfumed soap back home, but I scrubbed all over. I rubbed some of the soap on the little towel and tried to scrub my teeth. It didn't do much good. I even rubbed some of it on my hair and worked up a lather. Satisfied that I was as clean as I was going to get, I handed the soap to Mother and swam out toward the middle of the river.

I kicked and splashed and flopped around, feeling

not only the soap but all the nasty trail dust and the bad smells I had collected go floating away. I never knew swimming in a river could feel so good.

"*Get out of there!*" a loud, deep voice screamed at us. "*Get out now!*"

Startled, I spun around. A horse and rider came crashing through the willow trees near Mother. Covering herself, she dropped down in the water.

It was David. In one smooth move he pulled his rifle from the holster and jumped down from his horse—both at the same time.

"What . . . but . . ." Mother stammered.

David's blue eyes were wide. Frantically he looked around.

"*Get out now!*" he repeated.

Mother had her arms crossed in front of her chest. David was only a few feet from where she crouched in the water, hiding herself.

I was farther out in the river. Only my head and chin were above the water, but I crossed my arms over my chest too.

"*Now!*" David screamed at us.

I treaded water and stayed where I was. If that young hooligan thought I was going to . . . well, I mean, I didn't have a stitch on.

"I'm not about to get out!" I called from the center of the river. "Not with you standing there."

In a much softer voice Mother said: "We're not dressed."

David's hands seemed to shake.

"Please," he begged. "Please! *Now!*"

There was a desperate urgency to his voice. Though terribly embarrassed by his presence, and more than a tiny bit untrusting, I slowly swam toward the bank.

CHAPTER 11

David reached down and grabbed one of the brown wool blankets from the ground. He threw it at Mother.

As she wrapped it around herself and stood up, he never took his eyes off the river or me. When I swam closer, he grabbed the other blanket.

"I'm planning to use that for a towel," I said. "If you get it wet—"

Before I could finish, he flung the blanket at me. I glared at him.

I could touch bottom now. I got hold of the blanket and tried to lift it a little from the water so it wouldn't get soaking wet.

"If you think I'm going to come out with you standing there—"

Boots and all, he charged toward me.

I wrapped the blanket around myself.

Standing knee deep in the river, he stopped. "Hurry up!" he snapped.

I glared back at him.

"No!"

His blue eyes squeezed tight. "*Little girl*, you get out of there right this second or I'll drag you out by the hair!"

I wrapped the blanket about my shoulders, made sure every inch of me was covered, and sloshed to the bank. Water dripped from the heavy wool and made an instant mud puddle about my feet.

"If you think you're going to boss me around—" I cried, wheeling to face him.

I expected to find him right behind me, practically shoving me. Instead David was still standing knee deep in the river. Step at a time, he backed toward us. He swung his rifle from side to side, never taking his eyes from the water.

Mother acted as though she were going to say something to him too. But noting the way he ignored us and the intensity with which he watched the river, she didn't.

"There!"

The rifle snapped to David's shoulder. He took the last three steps to the bank in one giant backward leap. Landing between Mother and me, he cocked the rifle.

"There," he repeated.

My eyes followed the barrel of his rifle. A dark lump broke the surface of the water. At first I thought it was a turtle. Then I realized it was much too big. It was the tip of a nose—nostrils. Leathery and lumpy, it was a dark, dark green color.

Suddenly, about two feet behind the nose, eyes broke the surface. They were raised from the rest of the head on two kind of spiny lumps. Slow as smoke rising from a campfire on a still summer night, the rest of the body floated to the surface.

"Alligator," David whispered.

Lying motionless as a tree log floating down the river, it was nearly nine feet long. The only movement was the blinking of an eye.

A lump came up in my throat that I couldn't swallow. The alligator had surfaced in the exact same spot where I had stood, neck deep in the water, arguing with David.

My knees felt weak. For an instant I felt like I was going to faint.

David gave a little sigh. He lowered his rifle and held it at his side.

"Aren't you going to shoot it?" Mother asked.

David frowned at her.

"Why? He belongs here. We do not."

He turned and started for his horse. Suddenly he stopped and looked back at us.

"Next time you bathe, find a place where the water moves fast, where it runs white as it bubbles over the rocks. Either that, or a place where the water is shallow and clear enough to see all around. That way, one of you can stand on the bank and watch while the other swims. The 'gators don't like fast water. Neither do they."

With the tip of his rifle he pointed at a small clump of bushes about five feet to my left. There, coiled in the shade, was an enormous snake. It was dark gray—almost black.

My heart stopped when I saw it. Mother squealed and jumped back. She almost lost her blanket.

"What is it?" she gasped.

"Water moccasin. Usually won't bother you unless you bother them first. Poisonous. Might not kill ya, but gettin' bit would sure slow us down for a week or so."

With that he turned and strolled to his horse. He grabbed the reins and with no effort at all, leaped into the saddle.

"When you get dressed," he called over his shoulder, "come on back to camp. We have to get an early start in the morning, so you'll need some sleep."

As he rode off, Mother and I grabbed our clothes. We scurried away from the river to dress in a clump of willows far from the bank.

The minute we got back to our camp, Charlie and Les took off for the river. They had never seen an alligator before and were anxious to investigate the horrible-looking scaly thing. Mother and I hung our blankets over a tree limb to dry. Then we sat down beside the fire where David was stirring the beans that Charlie had started.

Although David still wouldn't talk to me, I found

out from his conversation with Mother that he had never seen an alligator before today either. This part of Texas once belonged to the Comanche. David's father had camped many times with his people along the Guadalupe River. David related some of his father's stories as he stirred the beans. Although scary, the tales about the alligators were most interesting.

"They'll go the way of the buffalo," he said finally. "The white man is never satisfied to leave things the way nature intended. He's always trying to change things—to leave his mark on the land. Someday, the alligators will be gone from here, and no one will even remember what they looked like."

He left to go check the horses. Charlie and Les came back from the river.

"Big ugly monster," Charlie said, shaking his head. "I'm sorry I let you two go down there. David had told me that those things were in the river. That's why I watched him so closely when he and his horse swam across this afternoon. I figured you knew about them too. I thought you knew to stay on the bank. It's all my fault. I should have . . . I mean, if anything hada happened to ya, I'd never be able to forgive myself. I had no idea. . . ."

Mother assured him that it wasn't his fault. She helped him mix up some biscuit dough to put in the big black pot that he called a Dutch oven.

While we waited for the biscuits to cool and the beans to finish, we sat around the campfire. Charlie liked to talk. He had eight children—six girls and twin

boys, who were the youngest. He had humorous stories about each and every one of them. I enjoyed listening to him. He had a warm laugh that made me feel
good inside, and I could feel the love he had for his
family in his words.

David and Les never said much. Neither did I.

When no one was watching, I eased my finger to my
mouth. My teeth still felt awful, and I tried to clean
them with my fingernail. It wasn't a ladylike thing to
do, but I couldn't help it. Besides, I was sneaky about
it and only did it when I thought no one was looking.

I was wrong.

Charlie stirred the red-hot coals around the Dutch
oven with a stick. Then he handed the spoon he had
used to stir the beans to Mother.

"They're almost done," he said. "Just keep them
from sticking. I need to speak to Tanita—I mean,
Amanda. We'll be back in a moment."

With that, he stood and motioned for me to follow.

I was a bit reluctant, but I got to my feet. When we
were far enough from the fire so the others couldn't
hear, he turned and leaned close to my ear.

"Forgot your toothbrush, didn't you?"

I sighed. I was so sure that no one had caught me
scraping my teeth with my fingernail.

"Yes," I answered. My shoulders sagged.

Charlie smiled. He smoothed down his long, droopy
mustache with his finger.

"You are so like my second daughter, Tanita. She
has the most beautiful teeth and is always worrying
about them. Come. I will show you."

He showed me how to find the thick, dry stems of grass called love grass. With the speed of a humming-bird's wings, he whipped his big knife from the leather scabbard. After slicing off a handful of grass and trimming it up, he put his knife away. Then he led me to where the horses were tied on our picket line. He yanked a strand of hair from Sarge's tail and began wrapping it around and around, about an inch from the end of the grass.

"Now," he said, showing me. "Bend the loose part up and keep wrapping, only don't go clear to the top of this loose end. Twist the hair around the whole thing, except for the end."

Suddenly the handful of grass was beginning to look like a pipe. The "bowl" was the short part Charlie had wrapped with horsehair. It turned where he bent it, and the long part looked like the stem of a pipe.

He wrapped the long part loosely with the horsehair. Then, squinting so he could see in the dim evening light, Charlie looked at the "bowl" part. He slipped his knife down a little to the right of center and cut away some of the bristles of grass. Then he moved the knife a little to the left of center and cut away more.

"Have to be careful not to cut yourself," he said. "Don't cut the horsehair, either. You do, the whole thing falls apart."

To my amazement, I was no longer looking at the bundle of grass that resembled a pipe. With the sides of the "bowl" cut away, the head of it was rectangular. The bristles of grass stood up about a half inch or so—now it was . . .

"A toothbrush!" I squealed. "You made a tooth-brush, Charlie."

I hugged him. For a second, I thought I saw his brown face turn a bit red. He smiled back and ruffled my hair, like he'd probably done with his own daughters a hundred times.

"You can only use it once," he said. "The grass gets wet and too soft. Rub the head on the soap. It tastes horrible, but it works."

I hugged him again, then raced back to the fire to show Mother my new toothbrush.

I liked Charlie.

If David had been a better hunter, we would have had turkey that night. We had beans and biscuits for supper. The next night we had biscuits and beans.

CHAPTER 12

And the next night we had beans and biscuits again.

I liked Charlie more and more with the passing of each day. He had to demonstrate how to make the toothbrush three more times before I could make my own. But finally I got the hang of it. He talked to me, too. It made the long days on the trail seem to pass more easily. As we rode he showed me things, like the tracks of different animals that came to the river. He pointed out the round leaf nests where squirrels lived in the trees. He showed me flowers along the bank of the river, and bright bluebonnets that lined the hillsides. More than once he called me Tanita, instead of Amanda. Each time he would laugh and apologize, then tell me how much I reminded him of his daughter.

As for me, I had to be careful not to call Charlie

Grandmother. He so reminded me of her. He was someone I could confide in. He was open and honest and neither of us had to hide or guard our feelings when we talked.

Except for the incident with the alligator, each day on the trail was less eventful than the day before. When we left Kerrville, David had told us to expect to be out for at least a week. At the end of two weeks, there was still no sign of the buffalo. I was beginning to doubt that there really were any.

Mother and I had become quite accustomed to life on the trail. Each evening when we stopped, we took a change of clothes with us to the river. We got our Levis wet, then rolled them in the sand. We would twist them up and pound them again and again on a rock. Mother said she had watched the native women doing their wash that way when she and Father had traveled on safari in Africa. We were a bit more gentle with our silk drawers and cotton blouses.

When we were finished with our washing, we would bathe. If the water was slow and the river wide, we would use the small white towels that Charlie had given us to take a sponge bath. We would use Charlie's Dutch oven to pour water over us and get the soap off. (This irritated Charlie a little, especially if he was planning to make biscuits or cornbread and had to wait for us to bring his pot back.) When we camped near fast-running white water or a place where the bottom was rocky and shallow, one of us would stand watch while the other swam and bathed. When we got back to camp, we would hang our clothes in the trees to dry so we could twist them in the bedrolls the next morning.

In the evenings we would help Charlie build the fire and do some of the cooking. We didn't really help all that much, though. Charlie took great pride in his meals of beans and biscuits, so mostly Mother and I just stayed out of his way. The last thing every night, Charlie would fill his big Dutch oven with water. He'd build the fire up enough so it would boil. In the morning we would fill our canteens with the clean water for drinking.

Once, during those two weeks, Les brought in a couple of rabbits that he had shot. They were good and a welcome break from beans. David brought in a small deer. It had sort of a wild taste that I didn't much care for. Charlie did a good job of cooking it. It lasted about three days, and on the third evening Charlie took his knife and chopped what was left into tiny, tiny pieces. Then he squeezed the pieces together to a size a little smaller than his pancakes. He cooked them over the open fire. I decided that was the way I liked venison best.

We didn't travel on the two Sundays that we spent on the trail. We made camp and stayed in one spot all day to rest. Charlie showed me how to catch fish from the river. We talked and laughed but never caught anything big enough to bring back to camp and eat.

By the second Sunday Mother had finished reading the two books she had sneaked into her bedroll. She busied herself with writing on the notepad that she had brought along. "It's not really a story," she had told me once, when I asked about it. "Just making some notes so I can do an article about our adventures for the newspaper. Or"—she glanced off wistfully— "who knows? I might even try to write a book about it someday."

At any rate, without a book to read and with very little paper left to write on, Mother spent more time with Charlie and me.

I liked that.

Mostly, what we spent our time doing was riding. All day long we rode and rode. We didn't cover that much ground, either. We probably averaged fifteen miles of riding a day, zigzagging back and forth—only to move three to five miles up the river. Nothing exciting ever happened, and it seemed that we were no closer to finding buffalo than we had been on the day we left San Francisco.

Even Mother, who was always full of enthusiasm and excitement, was beginning to have her doubts. One night, as we crawled into our bedrolls, she gazed up at the stars and sighed.

"Perhaps we're too late. Perhaps there are no more buffalo left."

Monday of the third week started out damp and humid. Usually the mornings were a bit cool. The air was fresh and clean. Today was hot from the very moment I opened my eyes.

My clothes were wet and sticky. Although we'd bathed the night before, my face felt gritty and dirty. I wiggled out of the bedroll and stretched.

Even the Sears, Roebuck catalogue felt damp. When I got back from the bushes, Charlie was busy at the fire. With a stick he scooted red-hot coals closer to the Dutch oven.

"Why is it so hot and sticky?" I asked.

Charlie's dark eyes flickered up at the sky. He seemed troubled.

"Storm brewin', I reckon." He stirred the coals again. "Best get your mom up and get your stuff rolled. We may have to do a heap of travelin' today."

We packed and ate breakfast. Charlie kept glancing at the sky all the time he loaded the packhorse. There wasn't a cloud anywhere.

Les rode on up the river. David crossed—the river was very narrow—and rode for some bluffs toward the west. We worked our way up the Guadalupe, just as we had for the past two weeks. With the exception of the sticky-hot air that seemed thick enough to chew and the droplets of water that plopped from the tall branches of the bald cypress trees, everything was the same. Just like always, one day seemed to blend right into the next.

My sixteenth birthday was less than two weeks away. For a short time I'd forgotten about my friends and Philip and all the fun things that there were to do back home. But today, with the heat and the quiet, my yearning to be home pounded into my heart with every step of Sarge's hooves.

If I were home right now, I would be planning a big party. Mother would let me buy a new formal gown— one of voile or lace, with a scalloped yoke and pearl buttons in the back. The servants would be decorating the entire house. We would have dancing at the party, and there would be cake and pastries of all sorts. I so missed cakes and pies. I even missed vegetables, although I had never cared much for them until this trip, where they were so scarce. At home, I'd be with my friends and we'd be laughing a lot and Philip might even try to steal a kiss.

Here—nothing exciting ever happened. My birthday would come and go, without notice. If things kept on like this, I'd probably waste away from boredom before my birthday ever got here.

Nothing exciting ever happened.

CHAPTER 13

A little before noon Les came riding toward us. He was kind of slumped in his saddle. His shoulders sagged, and he seemed tired and disgusted.

When he noticed us, he gave a little jerk. He sat up straight and held his shoulders back.

"Reached the headwater of the river." When he said that, his shoulders sagged again. "Just like David de-scribed it—big flat area, mostly rock. Bunch of little springs seeping up and branching into the channel." He took a deep breath and sighed. "Spent nearly three hours circling. Plenty of deer and wild-pig sign. Had a shot at a wild boar. Figured a little fatback to chew on or add to your beans might help the flavor a bit. Missed him, though. Anyhow, there's lots of game but not a buffalo track anyplace. Don't know where those darned things are, but it's for sure they ain't on the Guada-lupe."

My horse stomped his feet and stepped to the side. I pulled back on the reins, trying to make him hold still.

"Quit that, Sarge," I whispered.

Charlie looked over his shoulder in the direction that David had ridden. "Well." He frowned, curling the tip of his mustache between his thumb and finger. "Don't rightly know what to do. . . ."

Sarge stomped again and slipped to the side. I yanked on the reins, a little harder this time. Being behind Charlie, the packhorse, and Mother, I found it was a little hard to hear. With my horse stomping and wiggling around, it was almost impossible.

"No sense going on to the end of the river if the buffalo ain't there," Charlie continued. "If David's found sign, we'll have to double back." He frowned and twirled the end of his mustache again. "But if he hasn't found anything, then . . ."

I didn't hear the rest of what Charlie said. Sarge reared, but just a little. It was more of a bounce on his front hooves. I yanked the reins hard and slapped him on the neck.

Suddenly there was this strange loud buzzing sound. It came from the ground beside us, but before I even had time to glance down to see what it was, my horse squealed and reared again.

This time his front end came clear off the ground. His mane was in my face. I leaned forward to keep from tumbling backward off his rump. I grabbed for the horn, but he leaped sideways.

I felt myself slipping.

Sarge made two giant leaps on his hind legs. My right foot lost the stirrup as he jumped to the left. Desperately I dug my other heel into his side, trying to hold on with that leg.

He hit the ground running. Frantic, I grabbed for the horn. I touched it, but for only a second before it slipped from my grasp. I fell. It took only an instant to hit the ground, but it seemed like an eternity as I watched the brown dirt rushing closer and closer.

My right shoulder stung where I'd landed. Then inside my head I heard a loud *thump* as my right ear bounced against the dirt.

My whole right side ached. I moaned from the pain and rolled to my stomach, trying to get my weight off where it hurt.

The loud buzzing sound came to my ears again. It was so close it sounded like a dull roar. I blinked, trying to make my eyes focus and my head quit spinning.

Then—I saw it.

The snake was not two feet from me. His thick, massive body was coiled into tight rolls. His head was so near, I could see the hornlike scales that stuck up above his yellow eyes like the horns of the devil himself. A black forked tongue flicked in and out of his mouth. His tail, covered with little bulblike things, was raised behind him. That's where the sound was coming from—that tail that shook and rattled so fast it seemed to buzz.

"Rattler!"

Charlie's scream was loud and shrill. I thought at first it was Mother's voice, but it was Charlie. In the blink of an eye he and his horse appeared above me. They were so close I was afraid his pinto might step on my head. I started to roll out of the way.

"Don't move!" he screamed.

It was too late. I shoved my arm against the ground. Beside me I could see the snake's mouth open. Two long fangs flashed inside the pink mouth.

Above me I saw Charlie's hand reach for the knife at his side.

My eyes darted to the snake. He struck. His ugly head moved toward me as fast as lightning streaking across the sky.

I blinked.

CHAPTER 14

In that half an instant it took for my eyes to snap shut, then flash open, it was all over.

In midstrike, Charlie's knife had caught the rattle-snake square in the middle of the back. Less than a foot from my cheek, the angry head seemed to freeze for a second in midair. Then violently, viciously, it began whipping from side to side.

Long glistening fangs slashed. He bit, time and again, at the silver blade that painfully pinned him to the ground. Venomous fangs found the handle of Charlie's knife. He clamped onto it. Clear, brownish drops of poison formed at the tips of those frightening fangs and rolled down the handle of the knife.

Then there was a brown, crusty boot right in front of my face, and I couldn't see. The heel of the other boot crashed into my stomach. I was being pushed, then rolled out of the way.

When I finally quit rolling, I sat up. I held my stomach and gasped for air.

Charlie stood with his back to me. Almost as quickly as he had thrown his knife, he jumped off his horse and leaped between me and the rattlesnake. The snake's angry jaws released their grip on the knife's handle, and he began slashing back and forth again. Charlie stepped out of the way. The terrible sharp fangs missed his boot by barely an inch.

Suddenly Les was beside him. With the butt of his rifle he pinned the rattler's head to the ground. Sure that the snake couldn't move, Charlie yanked the knife from its back and cut its head off.

The body flipped and slithered. The angry jaws kept snapping.

My stomach still ached where Charlie had kicked me. My heart pounded in my ears. I tried to get to my feet. I wanted to run from the slithering body that flipped and flopped on the ground and the vicious jaws that kept snapping open and shut.

Every one of my muscles trembled and quivered. I couldn't move.

Charlie slipped his knife back into the scabbard and moved toward me, but Mother reached me first. I felt her hands under my arms, lifting me up.

"You all right?" Her voice quivered. "It didn't bite you, did it?"

The only answer I could manage was a shake of my head. It took both Mother and Charlie to get me on my feet. My legs felt like jelly. I couldn't stop shaking.

"That was a close one, Tanita." Charlie gave a little laugh. "You're okay, baby. It's over." He tried to make his voice sound light and cheery, but the way his words cracked and trembled belied his little laugh.

The sweat rolled from his forehead. Drops of perspiration collected on the tips of his mustache. Mother wrapped her arms around me. She was shaking too. Charlie hugged both of us, and we all three stood there for a long, long time.

"I'm all right," I assured them finally. Now I could breathe again. I had stopped shaking enough for my legs to hold me. "Really. I'm okay."

Mother kept inspecting my cheek and shoulder, just to make sure one of the snake's fangs hadn't touched me. Les went after my horse, and Charlie apologized time and again for kicking me in the stomach.

I thought it was silly of him to be upset about such a thing. After all, he'd just saved my life.

It had been a terrifying experience. But after watching Mother and Charlie for a time, I figured they were more scared than I was. I didn't have time to get scared. Everything happened so quickly, I didn't even think about what might have happened, not until it was all over.

Once, I leaned to the side so I could see around Charlie. The snake's angry mouth kept opening and closing. Much slower than before, his body kept wiggling and twitching, too.

"It's dead?"

Charlie glanced over his shoulder.

"It's dead."

I frowned. "Then why does it keep wiggling and biting?"

Charlie shrugged. "Rattlesnake for ya. Things are so mean and dumb, they keep trying to bite ya even after they're dead and gone."

He found a big log a few feet away. After kicking it over a couple of times to make sure nothing was under it, Charlie sat Mother and me down. He knelt in front of us and kept watching me to make sure I wasn't hurt.

Les came back with my horse. How far Sarge had run, I didn't know, but both he and Les's horse were lathered up and breathing hard.

"David's coming in," Les said. "Seen him top the ridge yonder. Riding hard. Don't know what's going on, but there must be somethin' up."

Charlie patted me on the knee and got to his feet. Before he got my horse from Les, he went to look once more at the rattlesnake. The body had finally quit wiggling. It lay motionless, belly-up.

"Rain," Charlie announced as he handed me the reins.

There wasn't a cloud in the sky. I frowned, not understanding. With a jerk of his head, he motioned back at the snake.

"It's gonna rain." He helped me to my horse. "Snake dies on its back, sure sign that it's gonna rain. Other signs, too. All day's been muggy and hot. Seen turtles and them fuzzy tarantulas crossin' the trail a ways back." He patted my leg again and apologized

once more for kicking me. "You've had a rough morning, Tanita. . . ." He smiled sheepishly. "I mean,
Amanda. Dang near got snake bit. Dumb Mexican
kicked you in the stomach. Now you're fixin' to probably end up wet and cold."

I smiled. Leaning down from Sarge's back, I kissed
him on the forehead.

"Thank you for saving me, Charlie."

His forehead turned a bright red. He smiled back.

There was the sound of brush popping and cracking.

"Get mounted. Storm coming." We could hear
David calling to us long before we could see him
through the thick trees.

He pulled his horse up. Yankee slid to a stop not far
from where Mother still sat shaking on the log. The
horse was lathered. White froth streaked down his
neck and chest. His nostrils were flared with his
breathing.

"We got to go!" David was breathing as hard as his
horse. "Storm comin'. It's a bad one, too! Found an
abandoned soddy about two miles over the ridge
there. Doubt that we got time to make it. But we got
to try."

Les brought Mother's horse and handed her the
reins.

Mother looked up at David. "Amanda was almost
struck by a rattlesnake. Sarge threw her and ran off.
She's all right, but if it hadn't been for Charlie's speed
and skill . . ."

"Please, Mrs. Guthridge," David cut her off. "Please get on your horse."

"Timber rattler," Charlie said. He went back to where the snake lay and cut the rattles off its tail with his knife. "Biggest one I think I've ever seen."

David's eyes scrunched tight. "Charlie!" His voice was a stern bark. Charlie spun and trotted to his horse while Mother mounted hers.

"I almost got killed," I snapped. "A huge rattle-snake almost bit me, and you could care less. I can't believe that you . . ."

"I saw the snake when I rode up," David snapped right back. "I also saw that Charlie had taken care of him and that everybody was okay." He stood up in his stirrups and leaned forward, glaring at me right in the eye. "You can tell me your little story later. Right now we got to get moving." He spun his horse and started off. "We're gonna be riding hard," he called over his shoulder. "Since you've fallen off once today, you best hold on to the saddle horn."

My eyes bored into the back of his skull. If I could have gotten my hands on him at that instant, I would have snatched every bit of his thick brown hair right off the top of his head.

I was so mad I wanted to scream. Of all the insensitive, rude, unconcerned . . . Not only was he too busy to hear about me almost getting killed by a rattlesnake, he had insulted me about getting thrown from my horse. That was it!

I stood up in my stirrups and leaned toward him.

"What's wrong? Big bad Indian brave afraid of a little rain?"

To my dismay, he totally ignored me. For an instant I thought I saw the muscles under his shirt tense. Only he didn't turn back toward me or slow his horse. He simply rode on. Charlie and the packhorse fell in behind him, then Mother, then me. Les brought up the rear. We moved off at a trot, but once we crossed the river, David spurred Yankee to a gallop.

I couldn't stand David! What had happened to me was terrifying. It was important. David didn't care a thing for me. His only concern was the rain from a little Texas storm.

I learned later that in a little Texas thunderstorm, there's more to worry about than getting wet.

CHAPTER 15

Single file, we charged through small thickets, dodged around cedar trees and rocks, following David toward the ridge.

A couple of times I thought I heard a low rumbling sound, like a far-distant thunder. But with all the racket from six horses snapping twigs and scattering rocks under their hooves, it was hard to tell.

At the base of the ridge, I expected David to slow the horses to a walk. It was a steep climb and there were a lot of loose stones. Instead, he charged up it, driving Yankee even harder than before.

Sarge tripped and stumbled as he clambered over the rocks. I didn't blame him for throwing me before. If I had seen the rattlesnake, I would have run too. I'd grown fond of Sarge, and I was afraid he might get hurt, trying to run up this steep grade. Still, for a second I thought about changing my horse's name from Sarge to David. That way I could at least get a little enjoyment out of kicking him.

I started to slow once, but Les's horse was right on our rump. I kept kicking Sarge. He stumbled and almost went to his knees.

Charlie's packhorse began to pull back on the lead rope. The gap between him and David grew. At a wide spot in the trail, Charlie motioned Mother to go around him. A bit farther up the ridge he waved me around too.

Finally, we reached the top.

That's when I saw it—an enormous, blue-green cloud.

Down in the valley of the Guadalupe, it had been hidden from our sight by the thick cypress trees and the hills. Here, on top of the ridge, the cloud was so big it blacked out half the sky.

The front of it seemed to roll and tumble like a log going down a hill. From here I could hear thunder, too—a loud, deep rumbling sound that never seemed to stop. A bolt of lightning slashed across the sky. It went straight up and down and was as big around as one of the cypress trees back on the river. Then a loud *bang* hit my ears. It wasn't the rumbling sound of rolling thunder. It was sharp. Loud. Angry. It shook my chest. It shook the leaves of the little mesquite trees beside me. I hated loud noises. My stomach seemed to roll with the thunder. I felt queasy.

David pulled his horse to a stop. Mother drew up

beside him and I beside her. Another flash of light came from the huge cloud. It was so bright, I had to blink. David sat completely still. I watched him as he counted to ten, his voice a whisper.

The loud *crack* came. Again it rattled my chest. It made the chills race up my spine.

"Two miles," he muttered. "We'll never make it."

He looked behind us. Charlie and the packhorse topped the ridge. David waved at him to hurry. While Charlie and Les were catching up to us, David jumped from his horse and untied his bedroll.

Charlie pulled his horse to a stop beside me. David glanced up at him.

"Knife!"

Charlie slipped the knife from his scabbard and pitched it across Mother and me. It was a gentle toss, and David caught it by the handle. He felt around with his other hand for the center of the two blankets. Then, with the knife, he made a slit right in their middle.

I frowned, wondering why he was cutting up two perfectly good blankets. But before I had much time to wonder, he told Mother to take off her hat. He had her lean down as he slipped the blankets over her. When her head appeared through the hole he had cut, he took her hat and pulled it down hard on her head.

"Knife!" he barked again. He pitched the knife back to Charlie. Charlie had climbed down from his horse and untied his bedroll. He caught the knife and slit his blankets, too. Then he had me take off my hat.

There wasn't time for me to say a word before he stuffed my head through the hole in the blankets and pulled my hat out of my hands. While I was leaning toward him, he smoothed the blankets and shoved the hat down on my head. He pushed it so hard that my ears folded almost in half.

Then both men were on their horses.

"Charlie!" David called above the constant, chest-shaking sound of the thunder. "You fall behind, leave the packhorse. We can always come back for him. Let's ride!"

With that, we charged on again. This time, it wasn't a gallop. This time it was a dead-out run. The blankets flopped around me. The ends popped behind me in the wind. We crossed the flat at the top of the ridge and raced through a little valley, then over the top of another small hill.

The storm was closer now. I could smell the rain. Even beneath the blankets I felt a sudden coolness. It was almost cold. A drop of rain thumped on my hat. Then another.

I tilted my head to the side so I could see out from beneath the wide brim. The blue-green cloud wasn't over us yet. I wondered where the rain was coming from.

We had only ridden a mile when the wind hit. Then—I knew where the rain was coming from.

It was a roaring wind, a wind that pushed the rain far in front of it, a wind that whipped the little cedar trees and leaned them over to the side. Beneath me,

I could even feel Sarge leaning into it. Running, he struggled against the fierce gust that struck us. Then there were more drops of rain thumping my hat.

We came to a wide, flat area with nothing but grass. The wind whipped and rustled the long dry stems. From under my brim, I glanced up at the storm again.

The rolling, tumbling part at the front of the cloud was right on top of us now. It was so close that I could almost reach up and touch it. A sudden chill of fear raced up my spine.

It wasn't a fear of the lightning that flashed in enormous bolts from the sky, or the rattle of the thunder that shook my chest from down deep inside. It wasn't the fear of the solid wall of rain that I could see coming toward us from the little hill next to the flat where we rode. It wasn't the fear of what might be lurking, hidden from view, behind that wall of water.

It was something more. Something much, much more. Something I couldn't explain. It was like things as insignificant and tiny and unimportant and fragile as mere humans didn't belong this close to something so enormous and powerful and magnificent.

It wasn't like a storm rolling toward us. . . .

It was like . . . like the hand of God Himself, tumbling across the Texas hillside.

The feeling made me tremble. I wanted to get out of here. I wanted to go home.

The wall of water hit us. Ahead of me I could barely see David. The rain came down in sheets. Like waves on the beach in California, sheet after sheet of water swept over us. Within seconds I was soaked. From the hat on my head and the two thick blankets that covered my back clear down to my underwear, I was drenched.

A sudden sharp pain jabbed at my back. I jerked.

Something hit me again. There was a loud pop on my hat. Then another stinging pain on my side.

Hail!

Big, round chunks of ice bounded about me. Solid and bigger around than the end of my thumb, they hit the ground with such force that they bounced up in the air. Like marbles being dropped on a wood floor, the hail scampered everywhere.

Again and again it stung my back. Even through the blankets, it hurt something fierce. I could only imagine what it was like for David and Charlie. They had nothing but thin blue shirts to protect them from pounding chunks of ice.

Ahead of me, I could hardly see Mother. David was just a misty form in front of her. He leaned down against the side of his horse, using Yankee's neck to fend off some of the driving hail. The rain and ice were coming down so hard and thick we had to slow down. We couldn't see.

I knew we were going to die. The hail was harder now. It hit with such force I knew it would rip through my blankets. I winced from the pain.

I couldn't stand much more of this. I knew Sarge couldn't either. Any second he would fall under the pain of this driving storm. All of us would be beaten to death by the angry hail.

And just as all hope was beginning to die, we were

there. Before us a small houselike shelter loomed through the rain. It looked more like a large lean-to than a house. David jumped from his horse before he even stopped. As soon as Mother came up beside him he yanked her from the saddle and virtually shoved her toward the doorway. He did the same to me.

For some reason I didn't mind his rough treatment. I knew he was only trying to hurry us out of the storm. He was only trying to get us to where it was safe.

I raced to the open doorway on Mother's heels. It was dark inside. I couldn't see a thing. It smelled old and musty, too. Still, it was such a relief to be out of the storm. I heaved a sigh, thankful at last to reach safety.

A flash of lightning came. It was close enough and bright enough to light up the darkness inside the sod cabin.

I jumped. My heart stopped. There, in the shadows at the far side of the cabin, were two men. They wore long rain slickers that made them even harder to see in the darkness.

The lightning flashed again. I could see their faces. They looked dirty, crusty. At their sides they held six-shooters. They were aimed at me and my mother.

CHAPTER 16

David was right behind me. Blinded by the lightning outside and the darkness of the cabin, he couldn't see either. I stood frozen in the open doorway. He bumped into me, then gave me a gentle shove.

"Go on in."

He pushed me only a step or two. I leaned back against him. Les crowded in behind us.

"Lordy," Les said, shaking the water from his hat. "Ain't been caught out in one of them since I was a kid. That was a mean hail. Sure am glad to—"

Another flash of light came. Les stopped in the middle of his sentence. He and David saw the two men.

"Don't even think about it, boys!"

The deep, soft voice, as slow as syrup dripping over Charlie's pancakes, came from the darkness beside the door. I turned and blinked.

My eyes had adjusted a bit to the darkness. I saw another man standing beside the broken door that leaned against the wall to my right. He held a big double-barreled shotgun at his side. It was aimed at David and Les.

"Get your fingers away from your side arms. Come on in."

Slowly, hesitantly, David and Les took their hands from above their holsters and raised them over their heads. The man behind the door was bigger than the other two. He had on a black hat. A white beard masked his rugged face. I noticed all that in just an instant, then my eyes went back to the gun. I hated guns.

I hated the darkness of the cabin. I hated the storm. I hated being captured by three outlaws who would probably kill us. Hard telling what else they might do to Mother and me, but most of all, I hated guns.

With hands held above his head, David motioned us into the center of the room. He moved close beside me, trying to keep himself between me and the three men. Wet and cold, Mother, David, Les, and I huddled together.

Once we were inside, the big man looked out into the rain. When he saw no one else there, he shoved the broken door back to cover the opening. One of the men on the other side of the room struck a match. Light flooded the room. There were two candles on a rickety table beside him. With the match, he lit them. Holding his revolver in one hand and raising one of the candles with the other, he moved toward us.

"You two short fellas get your hands out from under them ponchos!" he ordered. "Bring 'em out slow and easy. Get 'em up!"

I did as I was told. The blankets about my shoulders were soaking wet and heavy. They seemed to pull down on my arms, making it hard for me to stand with my hands above my head.

Mother took her hands from under the blankets so the man could see them. But instead of raising them above her head, she took off her hat and wiped her forehead. She stepped toward him.

"We mean you no harm, sir," she said politely. Her long hair flopped in wet ringlets down her back. "We were merely trying to get in out of the storm."

"Lordy," the other man gasped. "It's a woman!"

I started to step forward too, and take my hat off. With his hip, David bumped me back. A quick glance from those dark blue eyes told me to stay still.

The man with the candle came nearer. He held it close to Mother and looked her over. Then he moved toward David and Les. David kept inching over, trying to keep himself between me and the probing, tight eyes of the man with the gun.

"My name is Mrs. Ruben Guthridge," Mother continued. "I'm from San Francisco, and we have come here in search of a buffalo herd that has been reported in this area."

The man with the candle gave a little jerk. His mouth flopped open and the six-shooter he was holding on us dropped loosely to his side.

"You're that gal the newspaperman has been huntin'

for!" he gasped. "That newspaper man in San Francisco has sent telegrams all over this area of the country trying to locate you. He's offerin' a five-hundred-dollar reward for word of your whereabouts."

Mother gave a little squeal. The hat dropped from her right hand, and she slapped her other hand over her mouth. She spun to face me.

"Amanda," she almost cried, "I forgot to telegraph your father from Kerrville. That was the last thing he said in his telegram—'Let me know when you get to Kerrville and let me know you and Amanda are safe.'" She buried her face in her hands. "I forgot!"

"I'm terrible sorry if we frightened you, ma'am." The man with the candle opened his slicker and slipped his revolver into a holster. "I'm Marshal Ted Benton out of Forth Smith. Yonder"—he pointed with his thumb at the man behind him—"that's Dan Park. He's a Texas Ranger. The man with the shotgun's Stan Garner. He owns most of the land round these parts."

The big man with the beard lowered his shotgun. The other man opened his coat and put his six-shooter away. Marshal Benton handed Mother the candle.

"I *am* sorry, ma'am," he apologized again. "We didn't mean to scare you. Just don't hurt to be careful, and you kinda startled us, bursting through the door like you done."

His face was wrinkled and weathered from the sun. He was dirty and rough looking. He leaned around Mother, and I thought his face might crack when he tried to smile at us.

"You boys put your hands down. Get them wet blankets off. Make yourself to home."

My arms flopped down to my sides. I couldn't believe how they ached from holding up the heavy, rain-soaked blankets. David and Les dropped their hands too.

Everyone seemed to smile. Everyone seemed to relax. I wiggled my hands inside the blankets and started to pull them over my head. Suddenly I stopped.

"Charlie!" I gasped. "He's still out in the storm. We have to go find him."

"Ain't no need huntin' for Charlie." The voice came from outside, somewhere behind the wall where the Texas Ranger named Park stood. "Charlie's right here."

All of us jumped and turned to face the unexpected sound of a man's voice. Charlie wasn't there.

Then his voice came from a different place outside the wall.

"These fellas really are lawmen, they ought to have badges." There was a pause and the sound of Charlie's voice moved again. "They ought to have a reason for bein' out here, too. Papers on somebody or somethin'."

The hail had stopped, yet it was still pouring rain outside. It was dark, but I caught a movement, a shadow that broke what little light there was, creeping through the cracks between the sod.

"David," he called, this time from the side of the

cabin. "I'll keep 'em covered with this rifle. You check 'em out."

Holding one hand above his pistol, David took the candle from Mother. The marshal named Benton opened his slicker when David drew near. He sort of stuck out his chest so David could get a good look at the badge. Park did the same.

"Papers?" David asked.

Marshal Benton smiled. "Inside vest pocket. You want to reach for 'em or you want me to?"

David nodded, telling him to go ahead. Marshal Benton produced a wad of crumpled papers and held them out for David. David unfolded them.

"Got an arrest warrant on a fella by the name of Spud Carlson," David called toward the wall where Charlie's voice had last come from. He unfolded the second one. "Got a writ to transfer him from custody in Texas back to Arkansas for a trial there, and . . ." He unfolded the third paper. "Got a wanted poster on him, too. Picture. Square chin and a scar on his right cheek." David smiled at the wall. "Picture don't look like any of these men. Think it's safe for you to come on in."

There was a long silence. Then Charlie's voice came from the other side of the cabin.

"I'm wet and cold, but I'd feel a lot more comfortable if that big fella weren't holding that shotgun."

The big man with the beard laughed. He pitched the shotgun across the room. David caught it.

It took Charlie only a moment to slip through the

broken door and into the cabin. He didn't have a rifle, like he'd said, only his knife. Once inside, he slipped it into the scabbard.

The big man beside the door started to laugh. It was a deep, rumbling laugh. It seemed to shake the cabin like the thunder had.

Then, laughing even harder, he offered his hand to Charlie. "You got the drop on two of the best lawmen in the country. And on me. Didn't even have a gun."

He laughed again, then took off his long yellow pommel slicker and offered it to Charlie. "Only been two people in my whole life what ever got the drop on me," he continued while Charlie took off his wet shirt and put on the dry slicker. "One was a hired gun by the name of Wade Eggers. The other was a Comanche Indian by the name of White Hawk. You're a top hand, Charlie. You ever need a job, just let me know."

Charlie smiled back at him.

"Heard of that Eggers fella, but I never met him. Do know White Hawk, though." He pointed to David. "That's his son."

Suddenly the men were the best of friends. They began shaking hands and talking and moving around the cabin. The Texas Ranger named Park lit some more candles. They laughed and talked about David's father, and the man named Garner told of how, when he first came here, they used to try and steal horses from each other. They talked about troubles they'd encountered on the trail and about people they knew or might have heard of—and they totally forgot about

Mother and me, standing cold and wet and dripping in the middle of the room.

Shivering, Mother turned to me.

"I'm sorry I forgot to telegraph your father," she pleaded. "I bet Ruben's worried sick. It's been over two weeks since I telegraphed him from San Antonio. I'm so sorry. I have to find a way to get word to him that we're all right."

I took my off my hat and fluffed my hair.

Then Dan Park was standing in front of me. With the light from all the candles flooding the cabin, it was bright enough to see. He was much younger and not nearly as mean as he had first appeared when he was holding his gun on us from the shadows.

As he came toward me, he swept off his big hat. Thick, curly locks of red hair covered his head like a crown. His gray eyes never left mine when he took off his yellow slicker.

"Best get out of them wet blankets, ma'am. We been on the trail for over a month, so . . ." He held out the long slicker. "This coat's a mite smelly, and they tend to feel a bit sticky in warm weather, but at least it's dry."

His eyes sparkled as he smiled at me.

I pulled the heavy wet blankets over my head and dropped them to the floor. I reached for the slicker.

Dan Park was still smiling at me. Only somehow his smile was different. His gray eyes danced and twinkled. It made me feel a bit strange.

I glanced down. My white blouse was wet. It was so

thin it clung to me like a second skin. I could see through it as if I were wearing nothing at all.

Suddenly I felt very, *very* warm.

Then David was standing there. He snatched the slicker from Dan and wrapped it about me. I couldn't help but notice how tight his dark blue eyes were, how angry and stern his face seemed. As he wrapped the stiff yellow material about my shoulders, his eyes never left Dan Park.

The Texas Ranger's cheeks turned red. Quickly, he went back to sit with the other men.

David stood there for a moment. He held the slicker about my shoulders. It felt good.

Marshal Benton brought his slicker to Mother. As soon as she took it he went back across the room. David returned to the others then too.

I felt very strange. I was a bit embarrassed. But still, I liked the way Dan had looked at me. I liked even better the way David had rushed over and wrapped the coat, and his arms, around me. It tickled me—how angry he had looked at the Ranger. It made me feel safe and warm. My insides almost seemed to flutter.

David was jealous.

CHAPTER 17

Once Mother and I had the slickers on and buttoned, we reached up inside and took our blouses and Levis off. When it quit raining, Charlie hung our clothes outside on a tree to dry.

In all too short a time he brought them back in. Mother and I dressed underneath the tentlike slickers. The pockets of my Levis were still a bit damp, but everything else was dry. Back in San Francisco, the servants could hang a thin cotton cloth outside, all day, and it never dried. Here, in the hot Texas sun, even thick denim was nearly dry in less than two hours.

When I was dressed, I took off the slicker and started to take it back to Dan. David jumped up from where he was sitting. He took it to the Ranger for me.

I almost laughed at the way he was acting. Only, I didn't.

When Mother took off her slicker, both Marshal Benton and Mr. Garner came over.

"Dan and I are headed back to San Antonio," Marshal Benton said. "We have to pass through Kerrville. That's where the closest telegraph is. I'll wire your husband and let him know you and your daughter are safe."

Mother smiled and patted him on the back of the hand as he took his slicker.

"Thank you so much. He will be happy to wire you the reward money you said he mentioned in his telegram."

Marshal Benton shook his head. "That's not necessary. I'll just let him know you're safe."

"He would want you to have it," she assured him. "It would make me happy too."

Marshal Benton shrugged. "In that case, I'll split it with Ranger Park. He's done nothin' this whole trip but bellyache about how poor Texas Ranger pay is. Thank you, ma'am."

"I would like to offer you and your party the hospitality of my ranch." Stan Garner's deep, mellow voice seemed to roll through the warm, safe cabin. "Isolated as we are, my wife and children would love the company. You're welcome to stay as long as you want."

"Perhaps for a day or so." Mother smiled. "We could use the rest. Then we must press on. We have to find the buffalo."

Mr. Garner shook his head. "No need. We know where they are. Saw them yesterday."

Mother's face brightened.

"There's only about eighteen of the woolly beasts left, but they're in a little valley over on the Frio River. We spotted them yesterday afternoon when we stopped to water our horses. Good grass and water, so if this storm didn't spook them, they'll be in the same spot for a while. It's only a day's ride from the ranch house, too. I'll even get my hands to help you round them up when your wagons and lumber arrive."

Mother wrapped her arms around Mr. Garner's neck and kissed him right on the cheek. Then, squealing and jumping up and down like a little schoolgirl, she hugged me.

"Isn't that marvelous news, Amanda? He knows where they are. We've found the buffalo. Isn't it wonderful!"

"Yes, Mother," I answered, trying to calm her. I wished she wouldn't embarrass me by acting so silly and childish. "I'm glad that we've finally found them."

We went out and got our horses. Before the two lawmen parted company with us, Dan Park rode over. He brought his horse right up next to Sarge and me. With a broad sweeping motion he removed his hat and bowed.

"It was indeed a pleasure to meet you, Miss Guthridge."

He seemed to stretch out the word *pleasure*. I felt myself blush.

"Hope you and your mother find your buffalo, and I hope you have a safe and pleasant journey." He put his hat back on and glanced over his shoulder at David.

"Keep a watchful eye on the boy over there. You're a very attractive young woman. I think he's got eyes for you."

Dan Park winked at me. I nodded, and without realizing it I winked back. I felt my cheeks turn red again.

"Attractive young *woman.*" His words clung to my ears as tight and sweet as honey sticks to the comb. His words made my insides tingle. I sat up very proud and straight on Sarge's back. I liked it even more that he had noticed how David was acting. Before, as far as I knew, David had no interest in me whatsoever. In fact, I didn't even think he liked me. But the way he acted back in the cabin . . .

It was all I could think about. I didn't pay any attention to the scenery as we rode to Mr. Garner's ranch. I didn't remember that we hadn't eaten all day. I didn't even think about the raging storm as it roared and tumbled away in the distance. I just smiled to myself and thought about how protective and jealous David had acted. I remembered how his deep blue eyes turned almost black when he glared at Dan Park. I sighed as I thought about how he'd held me for a time after he'd wrapped the slicker around me with his brown, strong arms.

Maybe this trip wasn't such a bad idea after all.

I was startled when we topped a little hill and saw the Garner ranch in the valley before us. I was startled because it was sunset, yet it seemed like we'd only been on the trail for a few minutes. I was startled because the house was so big and nice and I had expected to see nothing so grand this far from civilization. I was startled by all the houses and barns and buildings around it, because it seemed more like a small town than a ranch.

And, if I was startled by the outside of the Garner ranch, I was downright shocked when we got inside.

CHAPTER 18

Mrs. Garner met us at the front door. She was a tall, slender Mexican woman with dark eyes and black hair. I could tell that she was most excited and happy to see her husband, but when she noticed he had brought guests, she remained quite reserved and formal.

A girl about my age, dressed in a blue cotton blouse and skirt, followed her to the front porch. Mrs. Garner instructed her to go tell someone named Stella that there would be guests for supper. Then as the girl scurried off Mrs. Garner gave her husband a little kiss on the cheek and introduced herself to us. Her name was Rosa.

She'd just barely had time to tell us her name when two children appeared at the open doorway. A girl of nine or so and a little boy of six came charging through the opening. Not nearly as reserved as their mother, they leaped for Mr. Garner. Somehow he caught one in each arm and held them as they hugged and kissed him and shouted, "Daddy, Daddy, Daddy!" He kissed them back and laughed—that deep, rolling laugh. Then he set them down, patted both on the bottom, and told them to go help Stella with supper.

Obediently they raced off. Mr. Garner introduced everyone to his wife. I was amazed how he could remember all of our names. She motioned us to come in.

"Allow me to give you a *very* brief tour of the house so you'll feel a bit more at home." Her eyes danced when she smiled. "Then I'll show you to your rooms. You must be exhausted from so long on the trail."

David, Les, and Charlie sort of hesitated at the door.

"You want to show us where the bunkhouse is, sir?" David asked.

Mr. Garner made a sort of snorting sound. "When I invited you to be my guests," he said, "I invited *all* of you. Besides, we don't have a bunkhouse. All the hands that work for me are family men. Each has his own house. Y'all will stay with us. Got plenty of rooms in this old shack."

The huge house had an elegance that was beyond belief. The furnishings were as new and lovely as anything I had seen on Nob Hill. There were paintings on the walls, fine paintings of high quality. Sculptures of marble lined the entryway and were tastefully placed about the large living room. To our left as we came in was the music room. A huge grand piano stood in the center of the room. Beside it was a harp, covered with gold inlay.

Mrs. Garner pointed down a long hall. "Study, library, and kitchen are down that way. I'll show them to you later. Now, I know you'd love to knock some of that trail dust off. I'll take you to your rooms."

A double staircase of dark red mahogany swept down on both sides of the entry. We climbed the tall, elegant staircase, and at the top Mr. Garner had the men follow him to the right. We followed Mrs. Garner to the left.

A ways down the hall, she opened a door.

"This is your room," she said to Mother.

"Oh, how beautiful," Mother gasped. She rushed into the large bedroom. Mrs. Garner and I followed her, and when I got inside, I could see what all Mother's excitement was about.

A brass bed was against the far wall of the bedroom. It was an enormous thing with a huge, overstuffed goose-down quilt.

"A real bed!" Mother squealed. "It's been so long. I can't believe it."

She dropped her bedroll on the floor and leaped on top of the mattress.

"Springs!" Mother almost screamed.

Mrs. Garner laughed.

"I know how you feel, dear," she said. "I've spent a few weeks on the trail myself over the last forty years." She nudged me with her elbow. "Come on, Amanda. I'll show you to your room. It's right next door."

We walked through a bathroom between the two bedrooms. It had a sink, with taps for hot and cold water; a porcelain stool; and a big, cast-iron tub.

My heart fluttered at the thought of a hot bath.

My room, though not quite as large as Mother's, was much, much nicer. It was painted pink, and there were crisp, clean pink drapes on the windows. There was a large pink carpet on the hardwood floor and a big, overstuffed pink quilt on my bed. I loved it.

"A bathtub!" I heard Mother shriek behind us. "A real bathtub."

Rosa and I went back to the bathroom. She leaned over and put a rubber stopper in the drain of the tub. Then she turned on the faucet with the blue *H* on the handle.

"You won't have to wait for someone to heat water and bring it up." Rosa smiled proudly. "Along with being a loving husband and father, Mr. Garner is also quite an accomplished engineer. Behind the house, there are ten water towers. My husband built them wide and shallow. He then covered the bottoms with black tar and black paint to help absorb heat from the sun. The pump works off a couple of windmills he built. Except during the coldest days of winter, we always have more than enough hot water."

Mother could only shake her head. "I am indeed impressed."

Before Mrs. Garner left us, she took a long, hard look at Mother.

"We're about the same size." She nodded. Then she

looked around Mother at me. Her eyes squinted as she studied me for a moment. "Think we can find you something to wear too, Amanda. I'll send Tina up with some clothes. Like I said, I've spent some time on the trail. I know what it's like to wear those rough, stiff denim Levis all the time.

"Oh!" She stopped and turned to us before closing the door. "Bathrobes are in that little doorway beside the sink, and you'll find toothbrushes and baking soda in the cabinet."

Toothbrushes! I yanked open the cabinet. "Yes!" My sigh was almost a swoon. There were two real toothbrushes. They had *real* wooden handles and *real* bristles. I brushed and brushed my teeth. The baking soda tasted much, much better than the lye soap.

I could have stayed in the bath for hours. But knowing we were expected for supper, I forced myself to get out and dry off. I slipped on a white terrycloth bathrobe from the little doorway beside the sink and brushed my teeth again. In my room three beautiful cotton dresses were laid out on my bed.

I picked the red one with the black lace. I chose it as a compliment to our hostess because it looked very Spanish. I thought she might be flattered if I wore it.

It was also quite daring. The neckline plunged in a deep V in the front and the back. When I pulled it on, I kept shrugging my shoulders to pull it higher. Then I looked at myself in the full-length mirror beside the bed. The red dress fit perfectly. The waist fit snug. I liked it.

David liked it too.

When he saw me coming down the staircase, his eyes almost popped. He smiled, too. Then, catching himself, he tried to act like he hadn't noticed how nice I looked.

Rosa complimented me on my choice. She also told Mother how stunning she looked in the blue gingham gown that had been left for her. The men had on clean white shirts and clean brown pants. Charlie's pants were a tiny bit too long, but all three of the men looked very nice and crisp.

Supper was lovely. A white girl and two Mexican girls served fresh corn on the cob, green beans, roast beef, lettuce, and carrots. We had real tea to drink and lemonade, too. David kept sneaking looks in my direction when he thought I wasn't watching. That made the meal even better.

After supper we went to the music room. We visited for a while, and Mr. Garner talked Rosa into playing the piano for us. She was very good. And she talked Mr. Garner into accompanying her on the harp, although he was reluctant at first. I was amazed at how well both of them played. The performers I'd heard in San Francisco weren't nearly as talented as our host and hostess.

It was hard to believe that Mr. Garner was the same man we had met in the dark cabin during the terrible thunderstorm. For all intents and purposes he had looked like some outlaw—crusty, dirty, with a scraggly beard and dingy clothes. Yet he played the harp like a master.

It was late when we left for our rooms. The Garners accompanied us to the staircase, and Rosa encouraged all of us to sleep late in the morning. She said that even if we weren't tired, her husband needed his rest. The buffalo would have to wait a day or so.

The three men went up the right side of the double staircase. Mother and I went up the left.

As we climbed, I could feel David's eyes on me. About halfway up the stairs I sucked in my stomach and threw my shoulders way back. I took a deep breath.

From the corner of my eye, I saw David stumble on the stairs. He didn't go down, but he had to grab the banister to keep from falling.

I looked straight at him and laughed. I guess I shouldn't have; I just couldn't help it.

Later, as I snuggled into the thick, soft mattress with the springs under it, I couldn't help but laugh again.

This had been the longest and also the most fantastic day of my whole, entire life. It would be a day I would remember forever.

As I wiggled my head into the big, soft pillow and closed my eyes, I thought . . .

This isn't Texas. This is heaven.

CHAPTER 19

Heaven only lasted four days. It was a wonderful four days, though.

Mother and I visited with Rosa. She showed us around the ranch, and we talked with some of the families who lived in the houses near the big house.

David and the others respected Mrs. Garner's request that they not do anything the first day we were there. Early the second morning, David sent Les back to Kerrville to find Pepper and the wagons. He and Mr. Garner rode off toward the Frio River, where Mr. Garner had seen the buffalo. Charlie tried to help the white-haired lady named Stella with the cooking, but she kept running him out of the kitchen. He seemed rather unhappy that he was stuck at the ranch.

For some reason, I felt no need to be grown up and proper. Though much older than Jennifer and Thomas

Garner, I took the time to play with them and some of
the other children who lived there. Tina, whose father
was the foreman of the ranch and who was closer to my
age, would join us when she wasn't busy helping
Stella. We laughed and giggled. We played hide-and-
seek and chase. Once they took me to a big barn with
hay in it. We swung from a rope tied in the loft.

And I loved the hot bath I took each evening and I
loved the feather bed I slept in. And I loved the room
with the pink drapes and pink carpet. And I *loved* my
real toothbrush.

David and Mr. Garner returned late the evening of
the third day. Les and Pepper arrived with sixteen
wagons, loaded with lumber, on the morning of the
fourth day.

As soon as Les and the wagons were there, it took
Mr. Garner only a half hour or so to assemble twenty
of his ranch hands, and we left for the Frio.

As we rode I couldn't help but marvel at the sight.
Before, there had been five of us, riding along the
Guadalupe searching for signs of the buffalo. Now, we
looked like a small army moving across the hills. There
were sixteen wagons, twenty ranch hands, and us, all
strung out, sometimes stretching from the top of one
hill to the top of another.

David and Mr. Garner led the way. Mrs. Garner
and the children had come too. They rode with
Mother and me. Behind us were Charlie and Les and

Mr. Garner's hands. The wagons brought up the rear.

We reached the Frio River before dark. Mother and I had a tent to sleep in, as did Mrs. Garner, Jennifer, and Thomas. The others slept on bedrolls or in the wagons.

The next morning, right after daybreak, David and Mr. Garner came for Mother and me. I barely had time to wipe the sleep from my eyes before they had our horses saddled, and we rode off.

We followed the river a ways, then at a sharp bend, we left the Frio and climbed to the top of a steep hill. At the crest of the hill Mr. Garner whispered for us to dismount. On foot we crept to the edge of a steep cliff. As I neared the edge, I couldn't help thinking how strange this place looked.

The hill where we stood was a normal Texas hill-country hill. At least, on the side we had come up. On the other side it looked like some great giant had taken a knife and simply cut the small mountain in half. The hill to our right looked the same, as did the one across the narrow Frio valley.

Mr. Garner put a finger to his lips and pointed.

There for the first time I saw the buffalo. Frowning, I tilted my head to the side. They seemed so much smaller than I had expected. Below us, they were not much more than brown lumps scattered across the valley floor.

I took a step closer to the edge of the cliff. I squinted, trying to see better.

Grazing and munching on grass, the buffalo seemed

no more dangerous or ferocious than the small herds of Mr. Garner's cattle. I had seen buffalo before only in paintings and books. From up here, they did not seem nearly as ominous as I had expected.

One of the buffalo was closer and seemed much larger than the others. I focused on him.

"Is that a bull?" I asked.

Suddenly David grabbed my arm. Pointing down, he showed me the loose rocks by my left foot. I was a lot closer to the edge than I realized. Gently he pulled me back.

"Careful," he whispered.

"Is that a bull buffalo?" I repeated.

David shushed me.

"Quiet," he said. "Buffalo are weird animals. When I was little, I watched from a hill while two hide hunters killed a whole herd. The loud sound from their .50-caliber Sharps carbines never scared the buffalo. They just stood there, watching the others fall, one at a time, waiting their turn to get shot. But the sight or smell of a man, the sound of voices, even the clatter of falling rock can send them into a stampede."

David eased me to the side of the hill. This was the first time he had really talked to me the whole trip. My skin tingled where his rough hand held me just above the elbow.

"Down there," he said, pointing to the place where we had left the valley. "That's where we're going to build the pen. We'll stretch a fence across the valley, there"—he pointed again—"and try to run them up against the fence. When they turn, we'll have some men hiding over yonder with solid wood panels to use like gates and shut them in." He sighed and let go of my arm.

I wished he hadn't.

"Anyway, that's our plan," he continued. "Oh!" He kind of jerked, suddenly remembering my question. "That wasn't a bull you were looking at. The bull's gone. There are only two calves. This time of year, with eighteen cows, there should be at least ten or more calves."

Even if David was talking just about buffalo, it was nice to have him talk to *me* for a change.

"Where did the bull go?"

I didn't really care, but with his excitement over the buffalo I figured it was a good way to keep him talking.

David shrugged. "Probably just wandered off. The bulls do that when they get old. They usually don't last more than two to three months once they leave the herd. Somehow they seem to sense when their time is drawing near. They leave the herd and wander off by themselves to die."

"That's sad."

I watched the way his blue eyes gazed across the valley. David really was fascinated with the buffalo. I wasn't. But I was fascinated with him. When he talked about the buffalo, there was a dreamy look on his face. His voice was soft and dreamy too.

"What about the calves?" I asked, trying to keep the conversation going. "Why are there only two?"

David shrugged.

"Like I said, the bull was probably old."

"So?" I shrugged back. "I don't understand. What do you mean, 'the bull was probably old'? What does that have to do with two calves instead of ten calves?"

His blue eyes fell on me. Instead of that dreamy look his eyes darted about nervously. I heard a faint gulping sound when he swallowed.

"Well . . . er . . . ah . . ." he stammered. His eyes kept darting about, never looking at mine. He cleared his throat. "Well, never mind. Come on. We need to get to work on the corral."

I frowned, still not understanding what I'd said or done that bothered him. He turned and started toward the horses. I followed him.

"David? What's the bull being old got to do with—"

He spun to face me. With his head tilted to the side and his hands on his hips, he looked rather disgusted.

"Go ask your mother."

Suddenly I knew what he was talking about. I knew why our pleasant conversation had ended so abruptly.

One time I asked Daddy where puppies came from, when my cocker spaniel had babies under the cabinet outside the pantry. He had said, "Go ask your mother." Another time I found a nest of baby birds in the hedge by our fence. When I asked the gardener where baby birds came from, he told me, "Go ask your mother."

Men are so silly sometimes, I thought, as I watched David swing into his saddle. Having babies was such a normal, natural thing. Why did men always get so flustered and nervous when they tried to talk about it? Why did they always say stuff like, "Go ask your mother"?

There was a part of me that wanted to chase after David and try to get him to answer me.

But another part told me not to. So I didn't.

Still, the way he acted so nervous and embarrassed tickled me. As we rode back to camp, I watched him and smiled a lot.

I never let him catch me, though. A few times as we rode, he would glance over his shoulder at me and frown. Each time he did, I would look very innocent and thoughtful.

Embarrassing David had been fun, but listening to him talk had been even nicer.

CHAPTER 20

For the rest of that day and the next two, the men worked on the fence and the buffalo pen. Charlie and one of Mr. Garner's men—a tall, slender fellow by the name of Trundell—stayed behind at our camp to do the cooking for our small army.

When Charlie wasn't busy cooking, he went down by the Frio. I watched him as he gathered mud from the riverbed and mixed it with dry grass. At first I thought he was playing with mud pies, like I used to do when I was little. Finally I realized he was building something. I didn't know what it was. But whatever the thing was that he was making, he worked very hard to get it finished.

Since the place where the men were building the fence was only a half mile or so from our camp, Mother, Rosa, the kids, and I would ride out on occasion to check the progress. When we were in camp, Mother and Rosa visited and helped with the cooking.

Thomas found a place up the river where we could swim. It was one of the prettiest places I had ever seen. There was a big rock that hung out over a deep, clear pool. Upstream, the river narrowed into a slender channel that cut a trough right through the center of the enormous flat boulder. The rock was smooth and slick. Thomas discovered that he could climb to the top of it and sit in the water. The water would shove him down the trough, swishing and sliding, until he plopped off the end and into the pool.

With all Thomas's giggling and laughing as he slid down the thing, it didn't take Jennifer and I long to join in the fun.

Mother and Rosa watched us. I had a great time with the children, but I was somewhat torn between playing in the water and listening to Mother and Rosa's conversations.

Rosa was a very intelligent lady. Like Mother, she had traveled a great deal and had seen many interesting, exotic places. Also, like Mother, she was a woman of strong will and determination. Once I overheard Rosa telling Mother how she helped her husband fight off a band of Apache Indians who had fled their reservation in the Arizona Territory. In my mind's eye I could picture her, rifle in hand, a determined look on her beautiful face, fighting Indians at her husband's side.

I loved the time we spent at the little swimming hole on the Frio River.

* * *

In the evening the men would come in from their work. Instead of sitting beside Charlie or Les and totally ignoring me, David sat by the fire next to me. We talked about the school that I went to and how it compared to the school he had attended in Pawnee. We talked about the ocean. David had never seen an ocean.

Mostly we talked about New England. I had visited Boston on a couple of occasions because Daddy's mother and father lived there. David wanted to know what the country looked like. He wanted to know all about the people and if they were different from the people in Texas and Oklahoma. He wanted to know about customs to see if things were the same there as what he knew out West.

I wanted to ask him why he was curious about New England, but I never did. I enjoyed his company. I didn't dare risk running him off by asking too many questions.

Each evening I looked forward to David returning from his work on the buffalo pen. I looked forward to how his eyes would search me out from the others when he rode in. Each time he spotted me, the look in his eyes made me feel like I had on that red dress with the black lace.

Mother and I were preparing to ride out Saturday morning to see how work was progressing when I noticed smoke coming from the river. Instead of following Mother, Sarge and I went to see what Charlie was doing.

The smoke came from the thing Charlie had been working on. Made of mud and grass, the thing was almost as tall as he. Dome shaped, it looked like some giant beehive, with an opening in one side and a chimney for the smoke to come out on the other.

"What are you doing, Charlie?" I asked, riding up to him.

He had been down on one knee, fanning the fire inside. Instantly he jumped to his feet and turned to me.

"What is that thing, Charlie?"

He smiled proudly.

"It's an adobe oven," he said.

I frowned.

"You already have a Dutch oven. Why are you making another oven?"

Charlie kind of stuck his nose in the air. "A Dutch oven is good for biscuits and cornbread, but there are certain things that I can't cook in one. I need a special oven for special things."

"What special things?"

"None of your business," he said, shooing me away with his hands. "Go on with your mother. I'm busy."

I frowned and rode off. It was the first time since I'd met Charlie that he wouldn't tell me something. I didn't worry about it for long. Mother was already on her way to see how the construction was going, and I wanted to be there too.

The men finished building the pen and fence by late Saturday afternoon. We spent Sunday resting, and planned to drive the buffalo first thing Monday morning.

Sunday afternoon we talked David, Charlie, Les, and Mr. Garner into going with us to the swimming hole. Rosa lent me a thick, heavy blue blouse. Swimming in my thin white blouse and my embroidered flannel drawers was all right with no one there to see me but women and children. With David coming, I needed something more, so I wore the thick blouse and my Levis.

We swam and laughed and played. We slid down the water slide. We jumped from another big rock into the pool. David splashed me, and a couple of times he ducked me. I tried to duck him back, but he was too strong for me to push under. David and Mr. Garner played with the children. They would pick them up from the water and throw them far out into the pool. Everyone laughed and hollered as they splashed.

I'd never had so much fun!

Tired as I was from all we had done that day, I had a horrible time falling asleep that night. When I lay down on my bedroll and closed my eyes, I thought about tomorrow.

I had fought Mother so hard about coming on this trip. I hated the thought of leaving my home. I had hated being away from Philip and away from my friends. Now, I didn't want to leave.

Tomorrow we would herd the buffalo into the pen and load them in boxes on the wagons. Tomorrow, we would start back for San Antonio, and from there, home.

Tomorrow it would be almost over.

I sat up and rested my chin in my hand. In a way I

wished we could stay here forever. But I knew we couldn't. So, I wished something would happen. Maybe something could go wrong. Maybe we wouldn't be able to catch the buffalo—at least not for a while.

CHAPTER 21

Yankee's ears stood straight up. He reared and pranced as he came toward us. He could sense the tension, the excitement in the air. He knew something big was going to happen.

Sarge could feel it too. He kept pawing the ground and wiggling around while I tried to tighten the cinch around his middle. Not far from where Mother and I were saddling our horses, David drew Yankee up and tied the reins to the limb of a small tree.

"Amanda," he called, smiling at me.

The way he smiled I had to glance down, just to make sure I didn't have on that red dress. He came up beside me and taking the leather cinch from my hand, tightened Sarge's saddle for me.

"I know you're a good rider. But . . . well . . . I'm not trying to be smart or anything; I'd just feel better if you'd stay here with Charlie and Rosa instead of going on the drive."

I looked at him. I didn't know what to say.

He leaned his arm across Sarge's neck. "Buffalo are dangerous. They're a lot faster than most people think. And if they ever turn on us, if they ever get 'on the fight' . . . well, I'd just feel better if you stayed here."

I couldn't say anything smart or cute. David was far too serious. I couldn't argue with him. I could tell how concerned he was, how worried he was about my safety.

Still . . .

I don't know why, but I had to be there. I had to go with them.

So all I did was untie Sarge's reins from the tent rope and climb on his back.

It took us over an hour to skirt around the hills. We came back to the Frio about a mile beyond the little valley where the buffalo were. Once we reached the river, we fanned out across the flat, a solid line of horse and rider. The wagon men stayed behind. They were hidden in a small clump of trees near the opening of the big pen.

We didn't have enough lumber to make a solid fence clear across the valley, so the men had cut cedar posts and made an open fence. The plan was that if the buffalo didn't stampede, they would see the fence and turn to the left, following it into the solid wood corral. Once the buffalo were in there, the wagon men would jump from their hiding place and close the panels.

It was a good plan. It almost worked.

* * *

Though they were excited and jumpy, we forced our horses to walk. We talked as we rode slowly up the valley. That way the buffalo would hear our voices long before seeing us and the horses and wouldn't be startled into stampeding.

When we rounded a sharp bend in the river, I saw them. In the distance, they had stopped grazing and had clumped together, sniffing the air. They were so close they seemed more like a giant woolly ball than a herd of buffalo.

Still as statues, they stood frozen, facing us.

Then, as if on some unseen command, they broke. In the blink of an eye the whole herd spun and raced away.

They were so big and ran so hard that their hooves sounded like the rumbling of a heavy freight train. The noise echoed from the hills like thunder rolling up the Frio.

"To the right!" David shouted. "Don't get in front of them! Try to turn them toward the pen."

The riders charged after the buffalo. Without me even thinking to kick him, Sarge raced off with the others.

At the cedar fence the first three cows turned toward the pen. The fourth buffalo slammed into it. Another crashed into the back of her and the poles snapped. Like water shooting through a hole in a dam, the buffalo poured through the opening and thundered off up the valley.

Riders drew their horses to a stop. Some cursed, disappointed that we had missed. For a second we all sat there, listening to the sound of the pounding hooves as the buffalo escaped our well-planned trap.

"Rosa!"

The sudden scream from Mr. Garner startled me. I looked over my shoulder. He stood in his stirrups, watching as the last buffalo disappeared through the hole in the fence.

Then he kicked his horse, hard, and raced off after the thundering herd.

Suddenly . . . my eyes flashed wide.

Rosa. Jennifer. Thomas. Charlie. They were all up there. All in camp. All directly in the path of the charging herd of buffalo.

"Charlie!"

I heard the scream, but it took a second to realize that the word had come from me. I kicked Sarge. We charged through the opening, right on Mr. Garner's heels.

Stan Garner was a big man, an old man. I couldn't come close to catching him, though. He drove his heels time and again into his horse's sides. I watched through the dust as he caught up to the herd.

"Rosa! Rosa!" he kept screaming over and over. "Rosa! Get the children! *Run!*"

CHAPTER 22

Mr. Garner waved his arms and yelled as he rode alongside the buffalo. It didn't bother them. They charged straight ahead, up the Frio River.

He kicked his horse harder and raced ahead of them.

Sarge and I were a good hundred yards behind the buffalo when we rounded another bend in the river. I could see the camp now.

Mr. Garner reached Rosa and the children's tent before the stampeding herd. His horse slid on its haunches and stopped. Frantically Mr. Garner's eyes searched. Rosa and the children were nowhere in sight.

The buffalo separated into two lines. Most of them streamed right through the middle of our camp. I saw the man called Trundell. Running only inches in front of the buffalo, he made a flying leap for the back of a wagon.

The herd streamed around the wagon where he hid, only to crash into the next wagon and the one beside that. The wagons flipped, and within seconds they turned to nothing but splintered wood beneath the raging hooves.

Three of the buffalo and the two calves veered off to the right.

Then I saw the little puff of smoke. I saw the dome-like thing Charlie had told me was an oven. I saw Charlie.

He stood between the buffalo and his oven. He waved his hat and arms in the air. He yelled and shouted.

"No, Charlie! *Run!*"

My scream was nothing more than a whisper, a desperate cry. There was nothing I could do to save my dear friend.

As I rode toward him, it seemed like a miracle was happening. The first two buffalo dodged around him. The calves did too. Missing Charlie by only inches, they raced on up the river.

I felt a lump in my throat. The third buffalo stopped, right in front of him. For a second she watched the crazy Mexican waving his hat.

Then . . .

She snorted. She gave one shake of her woolly head and charged!

I heard Charlie scream as the huge, massive beast

crashed into him. I kicked Sarge harder. I saw Charlie
fly backward and crumble against the side of his adobe
oven. The buffalo charged again.

Kicking and struggling, Charlie tried to get out of
her way. She pinned him to the ground. From the
place where her short, curved black horn dug into his
leg, I could see the dark red color of blood. Charlie
tried desperately to crawl away from her.

We were still at a dead-out run. I pointed Sarge's
head at the center of the buffalo's side. I gouged my
heels into his ribs as hard as I could.

We slammed into the side of the buffalo.

The crash was so hard, so sudden, the entire world
seemed to stop. It was like a fast freight train crashing
into the side of a mountain. Nothing moved.

The stop lasted less than a split second.

Suddenly I felt myself flying. I went straight over
Sarge's ears. Arms spinning, legs kicking, I flew
through the air. With a bone-jarring thud, I landed a
few feet away. Scared, frantic, I scrambled to my feet.

Sarge and the buffalo had gone down. Dust flew.
Hooves fought the air, kicking in all directions. Then
they both rose from the cloud of dirt.

The buffalo turned around and charged my paint.
Sarge was too quick. He jumped out of the way. Tail
and head high, he galloped off.

Then she saw me. Frightened and angry, she panted
for breath. Her panting seemed more like a low, deep
growl. Her black eyes cut straight into me. They held
me like a steel trap.

She charged.

I spun around, then ran.

It was no use. Behind me I could hear her gaining. It was like I was running but not moving. With each step I took, she seemed to close in on me. I could feel the hot breath from her flared nostrils.

Out of nowhere, David was there!

I saw him from the corner of my eye. He and Yankee raced toward me. He pulled his rifle from the scabbard.

The buffalo was too close. There was no time for him to aim. Instead, he threw himself and his horse between me and the charging beast.

Behind me I heard Yankee scream. It was a high, shrill scream, a scream of fear and pain. Then there was a crashing sound.

David's hat fell beside my running feet. I didn't stop. Something flew over my head. It hit the ground in front of me. David's rifle landed about six feet away. It blocked my path.

I stopped and turned to look back.

Yankee was sprawled on his side, feet flailing, struggling to get up. The buffalo dug a horn into his shoulder. He screamed again. Then the buffalo climbed over him and started for David.

There was no time for him to get to his feet. Using his hands to lift his bottom from the ground, he started crawling away from her. She charged, but David managed to get his feet up.

He shoved them against her head as she charged.

She sent him tumbling, then shook her woolly head at
him again. She lowered her horns. A hoof dug the
ground. Dust shot in the air like a giant plume of
smoke.

I glanced down. David's rifle lay at my feet.

The hammer was back.

I hated guns!

CHAPTER 23

I didn't remember picking up the rifle, but suddenly it was in my hands.

The buffalo snorted. She shook her woolly head. My finger went to the trigger.

David tucked himself into a tight ball. He drew his feet up and wrapped his hands and arms about his head to protect him from her charge.

I raced toward them. The buffalo lowered her horns.

With one hand I raised the rifle in front of me. The blue-black barrel was almost touching her side when I squeezed the trigger.

The explosion from the gun made a terrifying *boom!* The kick from the shot pushed the rifle back. It twisted my wrist.

The buffalo jerked toward me. Her side hit the rifle. Between the jarring shot and her body bumping the rifle, it fell from my hand. In a split second the buffalo staggered the other direction, away from me. She didn't fall. She staggered another step, then . . .

She turned.

Nostrils flared, her brown eyes found me. White froth dripped from her mouth. I could hear the growling, rattling sound of her breathing. I could see the hatred, the anger, in those brown eyes.

She lowered her head. I couldn't run. I couldn't even move.

With one step she was on me. Her woolly head slammed against my left hip. I felt myself lifted from the ground. I spun, head over heels. There was no sense of time, of direction—I just flew, for what seemed an eternity.

I hit the ground on my shoulder and right cheek. Dirt filled my mouth. The tiny grains of sand felt like boulders between my teeth. The pain throbbed in my shoulder and head. I rolled to my back and sat up. Frantically I struggled to get my feet under me.

The buffalo charged me.

Suddenly there was a shot. Then another and another rang out. I blinked and wiped the dirt from my eye.

David lay on the ground where I had dropped the rifle. He cocked and shot the rifle again and again and again.

Still, she didn't stop. Her charge was a walk now. Her eyes never left me. A step at a time, she kept coming. David fired again. He leaped to his feet and fired once more.

Less than ten inches from me, the buffalo dropped

to her knees. I scooted back on my hands and bottom. She lunged, struggling one last time to charge me, then fell to her side. My eyes didn't blink as I watched her. She breathed for a moment, then there was nothing but the sound of the Frio as it gurgled and bubbled down the little valley.

David dropped his rifle in the dirt and ran toward me. Before he got there, I felt hands under my shoulders. Someone lifted me from the ground. I looked around and saw Charlie. His brow was wrinkled and worried. Then David was there too.

Their words came so fast and furious, I couldn't even hear them, much less answer. They wanted to know if I was hurt. They asked if my leg was injured where the buffalo crashed into me. They wondered if I realized I could have been killed. The way they hugged me and held me up, I couldn't tell if I was hurt or not. They talked so fast and loud and shot questions so quickly their words finally blended into nothing but a solid wall of noise.

And above the noise of their frantic, worried chatter I heard another sound.

It was a soft lulling sound.

Leaning around David's broad shoulders, I tried to find where it came from. There, in the bushes near Charlie's adobe oven, I saw it.

The little buffalo calf was blond and ugly. He lulled again and tilted his head to the side as he moved toward the huge animal on the ground beside us.

My heart stopped.

The little calf came, cautiously, to his mother. He nudged her lifeless form with his fuzzy nose.

My heart had already stopped. It melted, then. Like butter on a hot grill, it ran down my insides to a little puddle in my calfskin cowboy boots. When I saw that baby crying for its mother—its mother, who I had killed—I wanted to die.

I had to get to him. I had to help him.

David and Charlie wouldn't let me go. I struggled, reached out for the helpless little calf. They held me. I fought, trying to get to him. I cried and slung my fists and screamed and . . .

David swooped me up in his arms. Charlie held my hands.

It had all happened too fast. The buffalo trying to kill Charlie. Then David. The rifle. Now, the baby buffalo, trying to find his mother.

I felt safe in David's arms. But my heart was broken. My only thought was to get to the baby. I yanked my hands loose from Charlie's grasp. I slugged David, fought to get away. David held me in his strong arms. His blue eyes were soft, gentle, understanding.

So I slugged him again.

Then everything started to spin. I took one deep breath after another. But I was shaking so hard, I couldn't get any air. A sudden chill swept through me and everything went black.

* * *

I felt cool, wet.

No wonder, I told myself. You're sitting in the water.

I blinked and looked around. Mother was next to me. Her arm was around my shoulders, and she was dabbing my face with a wet washcloth. We were in the shallow end of our swimming hole on the Frio River. I had all my clothes on, even my boots, so why was I sitting in the water?

"Mother? What . . . where . . . ?"

Mother patted my face with the wet cloth.

"It's okay, baby," she soothed. "You're fine. Just got a little hysterical."

"What happened?"

"You were kind of out of your head a bit, but you're all right now."

I felt very weak—exhausted, really.

"Did I go crazy, Mother?"

She shrugged. "A little crazy," she admitted. "But you're back to being yourself now. You're okay."

"What did I do, Mother? Please tell me."

She sighed. "Well, I don't know for sure. When I rode up, you were screaming and crying and beating the tar out of David and Charlie—"

"Charlie's okay?" I broke in.

"He's fine." Mother smiled. "Rosa says he needs some stitches in his leg where the buffalo gored him. But he won't hold still long enough for her to sew him up. He said he has something special in that oven, and won't let her touch him until he's through with it."

"What about Rosa and the kids? Are they safe? Is Yankee hurt bad?"

Mother dabbed at my face, then handed me the washcloth.

"They're fine. Rosa and the kids were up here swimming when the buffalo charged through the camp. They didn't even know anything was going on until they heard the gunfire.

"Yankee had a bad rip in his shoulder. Rosa got a needle from her tent, yanked a long strand of hair out of his tail, and sewed him up." Mother cocked an eyebrow at me. "I think that lady, along with playing the piano, has had a lot of practice sewing up wounds. Yankee's going to be as good as new in no time.

"David had a bloody nose from where you punched him. He's not hurt, though. Just more confused than anything."

I felt my eyes swirl around in my head. Then, suddenly I was more exhausted than ever. My arms flopped limply in the water beside me.

"Why?" I moaned.

"Why what?" Mother asked. "Why did you hit him or why is he confused?"

"Both."

Mother shrugged. "You hit him because he and Charlie were trying to keep you from going after the buffalo calf. You kept crying and screaming about all she was doing was trying to save her baby, and you killed her. I guess you were going to pick the thing up in your arms like you did with that little stray puppy you found that time in Boston. You were fighting them like a wildcat, trying to get to that baby so you could take care of it."

A tear leaked out of my eye. "We didn't mean to kill her, Mother. I didn't know she had a baby."

Mother cupped my chin in her hand and looked me straight in the eye. "You had no choice, Amanda. If you hadn't stopped her, she would have killed David or you or Charlie—probably all three of you. You both did what *had* to be done. There was no other choice."

Reluctantly I nodded. I knew Mother was right. Then I got to thinking about what I'd done to David and Charlie, how I'd acted, how I'd flipped clear out of my head. I felt so bad, I wanted to die.

My bottom slipped from the rock where I sat, and I slid down in the water. I went clear under.

Mother pulled me back up by the hair. "Now what?"

"Charlie . . ." I sputtered, spitting the water out of my mouth. "David. I'll never be able to face them— not ever. I made such a fool of myself."

Mother gave a little laugh.

"Like I said, Amanda. You were hysterical. Everything happened to you too quickly. It was life or death, and you did what you had to do. Then your feelings, your emotions, everything hit you all at once. The things that happened and the things you felt . . . well . . . they all got tangled up and spinning around inside your head and heart." She patted my knee. "We women *do* have the right to get hysterical every now and then. Besides"—there was a sly smile on her lips—"it's all right to act like that around men. Keeps them confused, off guard." She wiggled an eyebrow. "Keeps them interested. Now come on. We need to get some dry clothes on you, and you need something to eat."

I heard Mother's words, but I guess I didn't listen.

When we walked back into camp, I still wanted to die. I wanted to crawl under a rock and hide. I never wanted anyone to see me again. I'd acted like such a fool!

I hoped I could sneak back to our tent without anyone noticing. As we made our way there, all the men seemed to stop their work of cleaning up the camp to look at me. Most smiled. Some even tipped their hats as Mother and I walked by.

I couldn't understand. All I wanted to do was hide in my tent. I put on dry clothes and crawled into my bedroll. Probably I would have been content to spend the rest of my life there, if it hadn't been for Charlie.

CHAPTER 24

The sound of voices woke me from my long nap. I stretched and rolled to my side. I could tell it was late afternoon from the soft light that flooded through the crack at the tent flap. It was bright when I first fell asleep. Now the light was much softer. It was getting dark outside.

The voices came again. There were hushed whispers, people moving about.

"Quit pushin' me," Charlie's voice snapped. "I'm goin'!"

I propped myself on one elbow and moved so I could see out the tent flap.

Charlie was limping toward my tent. A red bandanna caked with blood was wrapped about his leg. He held something behind his back. When he stopped again, I saw Les and David shove him from behind.

"Quit pushin'," he growled. "I said I's goin'."

"Well, go on!" David chuckled.

Charlie looked at the tent. I could hear him clear his throat.

"Miss Amanda?" he called. "Are you awake?"

I took a deep breath, trying to clear the sleep from my head.

"Yes, Charlie," I called back.

"You reckon you could come out here for a minute, Miss Amanda?"

I kicked the blankets off my legs and sat up. "Yes, Charlie. Give me just a second."

I rubbed the sleep from my eyes and fluffed my hair. Then I struggled to my feet and opened the flap.

The whole camp was there!

Like a turtle ducking into the safety of its shell, I pulled my head back into the tent. Then I sighed.

Sooner or later, you're going to have to face them, I told myself. Might as well get it over with.

I took another deep breath and stepped out into the cool Texas evening.

Charlie smiled. He limped to where I stood. From behind his back he brought out a big tin platter. Right in the center of it was a cake. At least I think it was a cake. There were three layers. They were bigger around but not much thicker than the flapjacks Charlie fixed for breakfast. The cake was dripping with white icing. A single crooked candle stood in the middle.

Charlie held the platter toward me. The candle

flickered. Little drops of clear wax dripped from the tip to where the pile of icing had collected in the center of the fallen cake.

"Happy birthday." He smiled.

Everyone around us cheered and clapped. I stood there gaping.

They kept laughing and clapping, and when I still hadn't taken the cake from him, Charlie took another step toward me.

"I'm sorry, Amanda," he whispered close to my ear so I could hear him above all the cheering. "It was gonna be a right pretty cake. The best I ever done. But . . . well, when that darned buffalo knocked me into the side of the oven . . ." He shrugged. "Well, I think it musta fell. I'm just sorry that . . ."

He stopped and looked down at the cake. Then, he looked at me. His lips quivered.

"I'm just sorry . . ." The words were hard for him to get out. ". . . just sorry that it ain't as pretty as what you deserve."

His lips still quivered, and he clamped them together like a vice. A tear fell from his left eye.

I couldn't believe that anyone could care so much for me. The water started to well up in my eyes.

I didn't take the cake from Charlie. Instead I wrapped my arms around his neck. I kissed him on his brown weathered cheek, where the little tear trickled down.

"Charlie," I said. "It's the most *beautiful* birthday cake I ever had!"

I meant it, too. I think Charlie knew that. His brown
face began to turn red. A little tear squeezed out of his
other eye. My cheeks felt wet too.

I guess we would have stood there bawling at each
other if Rosa hadn't come to our rescue.

She took the tray and handed it to Mother.

"Mrs. Guthridge, would you cut the cake?" Then
she turned to Charlie. There was a gentle smile on her
face. She tried to hide it and look very stern. "Charlie
and I are going to stitch that leg up, *now!* You've put
it off long enough, sir. It's time to get it fixed."

She latched onto his ear like I had seen her do to
Thomas one time, back at the ranch when he wouldn't
mind her. Holding his ear, she led Charlie off through
the crowd.

"I'll bring the painkiller, Charlie," Mr. Garner
called from behind Mother. "Got a bottle of Kentucky
sippin' whiskey in my saddlebag. Ought to do the
trick."

As he trotted after them Mother made me blow out
the candle. I didn't tell her what I'd wished for.
Mother cut the cake into tiny pieces so there would be
enough for all the men. As they took the little slivers
of cake they thanked Mother and returned to their
campfires to finish their supper.

After a bit the Garners and Charlie came back. We
sat around our campfire and ate. We visited for only a
little while. Rosa could hardly join in the conversation
because Jennifer and Thomas kept tugging on her
blouse and trying to whisper something to her.

"All right," she said finally. "You may go get the presents."

It took them only a second to race to their tent and come back. Thomas handed me a wooden yo-yo. From behind her back, Jennifer handed me a brown package wrapped up with string.

"This is from Mama and me both." She beamed.

I untied the string and opened the paper. A red dress with black lace was wrapped inside. It was the dress I'd worn that first night at the Garners' ranch.

"It looked so good on you," Rosa said. "Everyone thought you should have it."

I wanted to cry.

"My present ain't here yet." Mr. Garner's voice rumbled deep and smooth. "Sent a couple of riders back to the ranch. They're fetchin' our best milk cow. It's gonna be my present to you, Amanda."

I frowned. My head tilted to the side.

"A cow?"

"Cow," he repeated with a big, broad smile. "You're gonna need her. You'll see."

Suddenly David was standing over me. He held out his hand. I took it, and he pulled me to my feet. He didn't let go of my hand as he led me across the camp.

Before we reached the river, he stopped and turned me to face him.

"You may not like my present," he said. "It smells bad; it's hard to take care of. It's a little on the ugly side. In fact, it's nothing but a bunch of trouble." A mischievous twinkle came to his deep blue eyes. "But after beating up on me and Charlie this morning," he said, rubbing his nose, "I figure you deserve it."

He led me a few steps farther. I could see a small wooden pen. No higher than my waist, it was some six feet long and about three feet wide.

Inside the pen was the baby buffalo. The white cotton blouse that I had on at the swimming hole was tied around his head to cover his eyes and nose.

I stood frozen for a moment. Suddenly David's arm was around my shoulder. His hand held my waist.

"He's a little bull calf," David said. "That'll make him a bit harder to handle. I tied your shirt on him so he'll get your scent. When we uncover his eyes, you need to be standing in front of him so you can give him this sugar teat." He reached down and picked up a leather glove. It was heavy, filled with liquid and drawn tight at the top with a leather strap. Sugar water dropped from the small hole cut in one finger.

Rosa moved up beside us.

"Lots of times a calf will lose its mother on the ranch," she said softly. "If we can find another cow that will let him nurse—that's best. If not, we do what David has done with this little fella—we find him another mother. He'll know your smell. He'll know you're the one who feeds him. The sugar water will have to do until our riders get back with the cow. After a couple of days, he'll be following you around like a little puppy. You're his mama now, Amanda."

David took me up to the pen. He warned me that the calf might kick, and not to get in with him until I'd petted him and gentled him down for a few days. He also told me that the calf might butt when I fed him the sugar water.

Then he took my hand and held it against the animal's nose as he untied my shirt from around its head.

The calf's nose was cold and wet. His little tongue was rough when he licked my hand. As I held the glove out and he got a drop of the sugar water on his tongue, he butted the glove so hard I dropped it. I snatched it up quickly and gave it to him again. It took the little buffalo calf only seconds to slurp down the water.

Charlie took the glove and went to fill it with more sugar and water. David scooted over beside me while I petted the calf and scratched him behind his ears.

"He's not a very good birthday present," David whispered. "He's going to be a lot of work. If you don't want to take care of him, Les or one of the hands will be glad—"

"Oh, no," I cut him off. "I do want to take care of him. He's the most perfect birthday present ever."

I wrapped my arms around David's neck. I kissed him right on the lips.

A sudden loud cheer erupted. David and I both jerked and looked to the side.

Neither of us had noticed that the whole camp had followed us to the pen where the baby buffalo was. Neither of us thought about Mother or the Garners standing there, watching us.

Really and truly, neither of us cared.

David ignored the clapping and cheers. He turned back and looked down at me with those deep blue eyes. With one hand, he took his hat off. He held it close to our cheeks, hiding us from the crowd. With his other arm he pulled me tight against him.

Then . . .

He kissed me.

CHAPTER 25

The buffalo caught themselves. After stampeding through our camp, they ran a couple more miles up the river. They hid in a box canyon. The next morning Mr. Garner found them. The men simply moved the wood panels they had built to block the opening of the canyon.

We had them.

The riders Mr. Garner had sent back to the ranch returned around noon that day, leading the milk cow. They also brought a large leather bag that held more milk than the glove I had been using to feed the calf sugar water.

I named him Potlicker.

He really named himself. The first morning I let him out of the pen to follow me around, he found the little pot that Charlie used to make syrup for our flapjacks. Before Charlie could get it away from him, he licked every bit of syrup from it. In fact, every time he saw the pot, he'd knock it over and start licking it. Charlie finally had to hide the thing.

Potlicker followed me everywhere. He loved me to scratch him behind his ears while I fed him. He loved the sugar water almost as much as the milk. Sometimes when we went to the swimming hole with the Garners, he would step on bedrolls or knock something over. None of the men seemed to mind.

It took three more days before we were ready to leave the Frio River. The men built chutes at the mouth of the buffalo pen. The chutes narrowed down to an opening, big enough for only one buffalo to squeeze into. At the end of the opening the men positioned the crates that they had built. Each crate had enough room for one buffalo and a little hay and water. It was so narrow the animal couldn't turn around. They had no room to charge the inside walls of the crates and break the thick wood. The buffalo still tried to break free. There was always banging and crashing and bellowing coming from inside the wooden walls.

After the men had the buffalo locked in the crates, it took twenty to thirty hands to lift each crate onto a wagon.

We headed back to the Garner ranch and reached it by Saturday night. We wanted to spend Sunday there, but David and Mr. Garner agreed that the buffalo would not do well in those tiny crates for very long. We needed to get them to the railhead at

San Antonio, then on to the ranch at Pawnee as quickly as possible.

When we prepared to leave at daybreak on Sunday morning, I couldn't help but notice how much smaller our caravan seemed without the Garners and their twenty ranch hands. Still, we did form quite a line.

Mr. Garner had two of his best riders lead us. He said they knew the quickest and easiest wagon route back to Kerrville.

They rode at the front of the line. The wagons and buffalo were next, followed by Les, Mother, and Charlie and his packhorse. I rode behind the packhorse with Potlicker behind me—that is, when he wasn't scampering around in circles or venturing out for short jaunts to smell the wildflowers he found along the way.

David rode behind me, leading the old milk cow.

As we left, the whole Garner ranch turned out to see us off. There was a lot of talking and shaking of hands. When Mr. Garner and Rosa came to tell me good-bye, I leaned down and kissed each of them on the cheek. "Thank you for everything," I said. It was more than Thomas could stand. Rosa lifted him up and Mr. Garner lifted Jennifer so I could kiss each of them good-bye too.

"Folks here at the ranch heard about what you done back on the Frio, Miss Amanda. 'Bout how ya risked your own life to save Charlie and David. And they seen for themselves how that little buffalo calf follows you around and how you been takin' care of him." Mr. Garner smiled. "They got a little song they want to sing you—kind of a little tribute to see you on your way. Don't mind, do ya?"

I shook my head.

He nodded at all the people behind him. Three men holding guitars started to play. A song burst from the people and drummed into my ears like the clickety-clack of train wheels.

> *Buffalo Gal, won't you come out tonight,*
>   *Come out tonight, come out tonight;*
> *Buffalo Gal, won't you come out tonight,*
>   *And dance by the light of the moon.*

And behind me, as I followed Charlie's packhorse and kept a watchful eye on Potlicker, I could hear Mr. Garner's deep rumbling voice singing above all the others:

> *I danced with the gal with a hole in her stockin'*
>   *And her knees kept a-knockin'*
>   *And her toes kept a-rockin';*
> *I danced with the gal with a hole in her stockin'*
>   *And we danced by the light of the moon.*
>
> *Buffalo Gal, won't you come out tonight,*
>   *Come out tonight . . .*

The song faded in the distance. The memory of the Garners, the others I had met, and the time I spent with them on the Frio River—that never faded.

We reached Kerrville on Tuesday. Mother instantly wired Father to let him know we were safe. We left San Antonio on Thursday, and by Monday the buffalo were safe in large, spacious pens at the Lillie ranch in Pawnee.

Major Lillie was most delighted to see my baby buffalo. He had procured the herd from Omaha, but of the twenty buffalo there wasn't a bull among them. Potlicker and an old bull of Major Lillie's name Blackbull were destined to be the fathers of the surviving Texas herd.

David promised to take care of Potlicker until he was old enough to join the herd.

"I won't have one of the hands do it," he said. "I'll take care of him myself."

Charlie kissed me good-bye when we left. "I'll make sure he takes good care of him, Miss Amanda." He curled the tip of his mustache between his thumb and finger. He gave a quick shake of his head. "I sure am gonna miss you."

I leaned down from the buckboard and kissed him on the forehead.

"I'll miss you too, Charlie."

* * *

At 10:05 on Monday morning, the steam engine puffed. The whistle blew. The steel wheels spun on the tracks. The train inched forward.

I was going home.

David stood on the wooden train platform. We held hands through the open window of the train car. As the engine began to inch forward, David took the big cowboy hat from his head. He stretched up on his tiptoes and gave me one last kiss.

Still holding my hand in his, he walked alongside the train.

"Remember, back on the trail when I asked you about the people in New England and around Boston?"

I nodded.

"The reason I was wondering," he said, clearing his throat. "Well, Major Lillie's been thinking about sending me to a school back there. I didn't mention it because I didn't know if I would be accepted or not. But Major Lillie gave me a letter saying I've been accepted at the Harvard law school next year." He was walking faster now. "Major Lillie said that learning the white man's laws and how to deal with them is probably the best way to help my people."

He walked faster.

"I won't ever leave Oklahoma Territory for good, and there ain't much here—a little oil, good farmland, nice people. It will take some time to finish my schooling, but . . ."

He was trotting now, trying to keep up with the

train. It was hard for him to run in those big cowboy boots. The train was moving faster. David was running harder.

"But . . ." he puffed.

The train picked up more speed. Hard as we tried to hold on, my hand was finally pulled from his just as we reached the edge of the platform.

"But what?" I shouted above the racket from the train.

"But I love you!" he yelled.

I laughed.

"I love you too!"

Then, at the top of his lungs—loud enough for the whole world to hear—he screamed:

"I love you, Amanda Guthridge! Will you marry me?"

He was so far behind I could barely hear him. The train whistle sounded again, and I knew that no matter how loud I screamed, he wouldn't be able to hear me.

So . . .

I nodded.

I was hanging so far out the train window and jerking my head up and down so hard . . .

Well, if Mother hadn't reached up, catching me by my skirt and pulling me back in, I probably would have landed on my head beside the speeding train.

"I love him, Mother."

"Yes, dear," she answered without so much as glancing up from the new book she'd bought in San Antonio.

"I'm going to marry him, Mother."

"Yes, dear," she answered, still ignoring me.

I hated it when Mother ignored me.

"I really mean it, Mother," I insisted. "I will marry David Talltree."

Mother peeked over the top of her book. "I know, dear. In fact, I probably knew it before you did. Now hush and let me finish this chapter."

My mother never ceased to amaze me.

We were halfway to Denver when she finished the book. We went to the dining car and ate. Then we walked around the train a bit to stretch and to check on Sarge, who was riding in the baggage car.

Mother picked up the other book she'd bought as soon as we got back to our car. Before she started reading she patted my knee.

"Sorry I didn't have a birthday present for you," she said. "Soon as we get home, we'll get you something."

I couldn't say anything.

After all the fuss I had made on the way out here, how could I? How could I tell Mother that she'd already given me the best present of all? She'd given me this trip.

Who—in his right mind—would ever want to go to Oklahoma or Texas? I remembered asking myself on the trip out here.

Now as I watched the green grass and the gently rolling prairie, I couldn't help but think:

Who—in his right mind—would ever want to leave?